DEVIANT BEHAVIOR

Earl Emerson

BALLANTINE BOOKS • NEW YORK

A Ballantine Book
Published by The Ballantine Publishing Group
Copyright © 1988 by Earl Emerson

http://www.randomhouse.com

ISBN 0-345-36028-1

This edition published by arrangement with William Morrow and Company, Inc.

Printed in Canada

First Ballantine Books Edition: August 1990

15   14   13   12   11   10

For Sara,
with all my love

He is a relatively poor man, or he would not be a detective at all. He is a common man or he could not go among common people. He has a sense of character, or he would not know his job. . . . He talks as the man of his age talks, that is, with rude wit, a lively sense of the grotesque, a disgust for sham, and a contempt for pettiness. He is a lonely man.

—Raymond Chandler, *The Simple Art of Murder*

1

"HE'S BEEN MISSING A WEEK," SAID THE THIN woman as the four of us walked into Kathy Birchfield's law office.

"At first we thought he was bluffing. You know how it is," said the man. "Sometimes you have to call a kid's bluff or he walks all over you. Kids are like that. Especially adopted ones. You got kids?"

"No children," said Kathy, smiling in my direction. "I'm not married." It was the noon recess, our appointment with the Steebs sandwiched between courtroom sessions. I had been with Kathy, sitting through a robbery trial for which I'd done a long and convoluted investigation of the prosecution's main witness, who turned out to be a classic flake.

After Kathy seated the odd-looking couple in matching rattan chairs at one end of her desk, she eased into her Italian leather swivel chair. The room was breezy and light, presided over by tall fig and palm plants and a bank of high stained glass windows.

Both in their fifties, the man and woman were Kathy's longtime clients Dudley and Faith Steeb. Neither of them got enough sun; their complexions wan and unspotted. If one were feeling uncharitable, one might call them geeks. The two of them grinned across the desk at Kathy, he

1

toothy and fatuous, she bashful and cheerless. He had wetted and combed his cowlick but hadn't come close to taming it.

So buck-toothed that he could barely shutter his dry teeth with his lips, Dudley had what was best described as a loud smile. It was incessant and, if you hadn't known him long enough, unnerving.

"Thank you for seeing us on such short notice," Steeb said. His wife nodded solemnly. "I know you're in trial with something important, but we thought you might hook us up with an investigation company or something. Our situation is rather upsetting."

"We're worried sick about our older boy," said the wife.

Sneaking a look at my disheveled form on the couch, Kathy said, "What exactly is the problem?"

"I'd better let Faith fill you in. I boil every time I think about it," said Dudley Steeb. "He's taking advantage of us. And this is going to cost us a bundle."

Whispering to her husband, Mrs. Steeb said, "You don't know how much it's going to cost. That's one reason we're here."

The windows faced east, looking out over green maples in Occidental Park, with its shuffling panhandlers, strutting pigeons, and, at this time of year, the occasional camera-toting tourist. On the street below, a girl bellowed her canned spiel as she conducted a tour of underground Seattle, the part of the city left after the great fire of 1889, when, instead of clearing the rubble away, the weary city fathers rebuilt atop the debris. Pockets of the old city had been left underground. Across the square, sunlight glanced off the craggy Pioneer Building built for Henry Yesler in 1892.

Kathy wore a navy blue business suit. Somehow she managed to make her gorgeous dark hair look conservative for these affairs, pinned up and back but not severely—sort of Our Miss Brooksish. Kathy had crossed her legs, was bouncing the free one. I watched a slim knee encased in a silky stocking.

"I'm going to punish him for this," Dudley Steeb said,

bluntly, bristling at his own statement. His grin had turned upside down.

Ignoring her husband, Faith looked imploringly at Kathy. "They haven't been any trouble until just recently. They really haven't. They were so cute and lost-looking when we got them. The boys are adopted. Elmore's the one. He's the oldest." She glanced nervously across the room at me.

Kathy said, "This is Thomas Black, my investigator. I wanted him to listen so he could give an immediate opinion. As I said earlier, I have to be back in court in forty-five minutes. As an attorney I don't find people. Thomas is very good at it."

"How long has your boy been gone?" I asked. "Exactly."

"Elmore's been missing . . . let's see. Last Monday. And this is Tuesday. I guess it's been eight days."

"Eight days," Dudley confirmed, inhaling deeply and making a ritualistic elbow-waggling show of baring his wrist-watch. He stared at it as if it had stopped. "Are you bonded, Black?"

"Thomas used to be a Seattle policeman. He's a private investigator now, the best there is. Licensed. Bonded. The very best." Kathy didn't bother to tell him that in this state a license was a simple matter of paperwork. I could see her debating whether or not to give him her standard cockeyed speech about the time I tracked down a Persian cat that had been missing for three years, but then I sensed she thought these clients and their predicament were too important for horse-play.

Faith Steeb was reedy, not quite emaciated, almost a head taller than Dudley. Her face was shaped like the back of a spoon. She smiled. Her teeth were capped, and the incongruity of those perfect porcelain teeth in that homely face staked a claim on my sympathy.

"Elmore's a senior in high school," said Faith. "Supposed to be graduating in a week. And we haven't seen him. Not at all. Even Elroy hasn't seen him. Just up and van-

ished." A single tear dropped onto her lap and made a dark
star in the material of her skirt.

"Elmore and Elroy?" asked Kathy.

"They're natural brothers. We adopted them. Elmore was
five. Elroy three. Twelve years ago."

I said, "So now Elmore's seventeen. Elroy fifteen?"

"Elroy's almost fifteen. In a few weeks. In school for
some reason they like to go by Todd and Buzz. Elmore's
Todd. Elroy's Buzz."

"Why do you think Elmore left?" I asked.

Faith said, "We don't have any idea."

I doubted that very much. "He leave a note? Despondent
over something? Worried about his future? Maybe he wasn't
going to graduate."

"Elmore's graduating," said Dudley. "I don't know
why they let them out with grades like that. When I graduated, I had an average of three-point-eight-seven-three.
Taking all the hardest courses. I was captain of the chess
club. On the debate team. Three-point-eight-seven-
three."

"He's got prizes," said Faith defensively. "For music.
And for track. He's good at what he wants to be good at.
They came to the house to offer him scholarships. They
wanted him at several schools."

"Nobody ever offered me a scholarship," said Dudley.

"Was his disappearance precipitated by a family
fight?" I asked.

"We've had a few disputes," said Dudley, avoiding
my eyes. He glanced at Kathy and then leaned back in
his chair, dropped his pale hands to his paunch, and
stared out the window at the pedestrians below on the
street. He had washed-out blue eyes, and when he wasn't
grinning like a stuffed rabbit, I could see they were
hooded and rather melancholy.

"Nothing serious," said Faith. "Really. Nothing serious. It's the suicide. That's the thing. We're afraid he
might try to commit suicide."

"I'm not," said Dudley. "He doesn't have the guts."

"The boy's uncle died six years ago," said Faith.

"Jumped off a building. Ever since, Elmore's had this preoccupation with the act. Both the boys have. I don't know what could be so fascinating. He's got books on it. Clipped articles from newspapers and magazines. Even wrote a report for school about mental health and suicide."

"The only A he got all year," Dudley Steeb said flatly. "Except music. There's no possibility of suicide. Been no suicides on my side of the family."

"They're adopted," said Faith.

"I know they're adopted," snapped Dudley.

"You don't act like it sometimes."

"They're adopted, okay? Adopted. Adopted."

Somehow these two had escaped the veneer of sophistication the very rich seemed to acquire. It was hard to believe Kathy's assertion that they were the wealthiest couple I'd run into all year. The sole owners of America's Carpets, they could buy the block I lived on and bulldoze it into a cat box on a whim. Yet they were the kind of people who never seemed to belong, as if they'd been routed at birth to the wrong galaxy.

Faith watched her own bony and knobbed fingers twine about themselves in her lap. Her clothing was expensive but not stylish. The jacket hung from her bony shoulders like a burlap sack.

She mumbled, "It was my brother, Jan, who killed himself. The boys were deeply attached to him. Nobody really knows why he did it. Everything was going so well. Jan and Dudley started the business together when they were still kids almost. Dudley hired me on as a bookkeeper, and we fell in love. We got married six months later. It's been twenty-five years now."

"I swooned her," bragged Dudley, the grin back in place, louder than ever. "I interviewed fifteen girls for that bookkeeper job, but I chose Faith."

Faith said, "Jan didn't have any reason to kill himself. Things had gone so well for him. Except the divorce. He got divorced about two years before. Maybe he was depressed. Or allergic to milk or wheat or something. They say certain allergies can trigger chemical reactions in the human brain.''

I clasped my hands around one knee. "The police tell you anything about your boy?"

"We've tried that avenue till we're blue in the face," said Dudley. "They get so many runaways in this town they don't even bother looking. All they told us was he'd come back. They said they almost always come back. He hasn't. I figure if he can stay away a week, he can stay away a year."

Or forever, I thought. I tried to figure out what sort of father Dudley would make when he wasn't so irascible, but I couldn't screw the picture into focus. I said, "It's easy for a kid to hide here. Or he could have left the area. Could be in San Francisco. Alaska's big now. Hollywood. You'd be surprised how many end up in Hollywood. Especially girls."

"I don't think so," said Faith. "Elmore's not a Hollywood kind of boy."

"What about his natural parents?"

"His father's dead," said Faith. "The mother is living in Portland. Both boys have met her. She has her own family and life now. I don't think there's anything in that. We called her, and she really didn't seem to know where he was. Their reunion several years ago was a little anticlimactic. Will you find him for us, Mr. Black?"

I surveyed the pair sitting at the end of the desk and then Kathy, who was chewing her lip, lost in thought, undoubtedly kicking around what she wanted to say in court that afternoon.

"What are you going to do with him when he turns up?"

Faith sat erect. "We're going to love him, Mr. Black. We're going to love him until we can't love him anymore."

Dudley stared out the window.

"Okay. Yeah, I'll try to find him. He have any close friends? Anybody he might turn to? Girl friends?"

"There was one," Faith said, glancing at Dudley tearfully. "He hasn't seen her in a while. There were a couple of boys he trained with, but we've spoken to them."

"Trained?"

"Cross country and track. Elmore is the fastest high schooler in the state for fifteen hundred meters. Plus, this was the third year in a row he won the state triple A cross-country title. Elroy was fifth. Elroy barely trains. And he's only a sophomore."

"Track season over?"

"He had a couple of summer meets scheduled," said Dudley testily. "Coach has a summer team he works with. Except Elmore had a falling-out with Coach Blankenship three weeks ago. Like a nincompoop he quit the team on the eve of the state track finals. Nobody could touch him in two, maybe three events. And he didn't bother to show. Revolting, isn't it?"

Faith spoke softly. "He's a different individual, Mr. Black. Got his own way about him."

"He's a numskull," said Dudley, without turning from the window. "Turned down scholarships. Sassed teachers. Sassed me. Mouth has turned into a sewer. He hasn't had a grade higher than a C in two years. I think it's hereditary. I think his real father was a bum. You know how he died? Shot in a hunting accident. I bet he was shooting up property or on a drunken binge and somebody nailed him."

"Elmore's not a stupid child, Mr. Black," said Faith Steeb, needling her husband with a look. "Believe me, he's not. Why, they gave him a test and said he should be in the top one percent of his class. His counselor told us he was performing far below his natural capabilities."

"Deviant behavior, Mr. Black," said Dudley Steeb. "That's what it's all about."

"Why do you say that?"

"We wanted him in college next fall. We thought he wanted it, too. Now he seems to have other priorities."

"He's had a bad few months," said Faith. "Lost his girl friend. Had that upset with the track coach and quit the team. And he's been thinking about his uncle Jan more and more. Poor Jan. They've even been bothering Mother about it."

"He's a deviant," stated Dudley flatly. He didn't seem

like a particularly demanding or hard man, though it would take a seventeen-year-old boy to test that theory. Despite his worldly success, I didn't see many stretch marks on Dudley's ego. I wondered aloud why he and the boy didn't get along, if there was more than he acknowledged.

Faith glowered at her husband. Then he turned to me. "I love my boys, Mr. Black. We both do."

"I'm sure you do," I said. The fact was, a boy who was loved the way this father and mother claimed didn't voluntarily hit the streets. I wondered what pressures had prompted Todd's flight. "You branded him a deviant a minute ago. Does the boy know you feel that way about him?"

"You don't know Elmore," said Dudley. "You don't know half of what's gone on. He's engaged in some bizarre behavior."

"Tell me about it."

"Nothing we need delve into."

"He means quitting the cross-country team and so forth, don't you, cupcake?" said Faith.

'Stuff like that.''

I let it pass and gave them my rates, which are not particularly steep, and in return was assured by Faith that money was no object. Dudley stared out the window as if to say money was certainly an object, but he'd address that when he didn't have an audience. They were holding back facts, but I would find out soon enough.

"How quickly will you have him?" Faith asked.

I smiled. "Sometimes kids are standing down on the corner of First and Pike with a sign around their neck that says, FIND ME. Other times they make it impossible. I'll need a picture. A list of his buddies and their phone numbers. And I'll want to talk to his brother."

Faith handed me a list of friends, which she had already prepared. The paper fluttered in her trembling hand. I didn't bother to ask if the boy was ingesting, buying, or hawking drugs. They probably wouldn't know, and if they did and he was, there was a good chance they'd lie about it. If it hadn't already occurred to them, they didn't need to be entertaining the disagreeable visions my inquiry would spur.

"Getting a picture will be a little difficult," said Faith Steeb.

"How so?"

"There aren't any pictures of Elmore."

2

CHAGRINED AT HAVING TO UTTER THE WORDS, Faith Steeb snapped and unsnapped the steel clasp on her purse several times before she realized the clickety noise in the quiet room was her own doing. "Awhile back, maybe six months ago, Elmore announced he was going to be a spy—that is, that he was going to pursue a life occupation as a spy. He said a spy without a recorded past would be preferable. Before we knew what he was doing, he'd systematically destroyed every picture taken of him after about the age of ten."

"You're kidding," said Kathy, giving me a look.

"I'm not. He did this."

"Sure did," said Dudley glumly.

"He make a lot of announcements like that?" I asked.

"That was the only one I can think of," said Faith. "Wait. He said he was going to win the state championships before that first time, too. But he did win. By almost twenty-five seconds."

"Blankenship said he'd never seen an athlete like him," added Dudley proudly. It was the first time I'd heard pride creep into his voice.

"Planning to be a spy?"

"CIA," said Dudley.

10

"School pictures? Maybe we could get another print from the company."

"Elmore hasn't had a school picture taken in years. He just wasn't interested in lining up with the rest of the sheep, as he termed it."

"What about the negatives of the pictures you must have taken over the years?"

"The negatives disappeared when the pictures did," said Faith.

Still looking out the windows, Dudley bobbled his eyebrows in an I-told-you-so gesture.

"He is a sweet boy," said Faith, displaying the slavish loyalty that was both her right and duty. She handed me a snapshot that had spent some years pressed in a wallet. It smelled like a dollar bill. "This was taken in fourth grade. Actually he doesn't look all that different. Blue eyes. Five-foot-nine. A hundred and thirty-five pounds. There is some scarring on one side of his face." The way she said this last served as a warning for me not to ask about it.

I didn't. In a week I would know more about her boy than she did.

The younger son, Elroy, aka Buzz, had promised to remain home after school in case I wanted to interrogate him. I did. I figured the little brother would know Elmore's haunts better than anyone. And I could drive him around for some preliminary scouting, although I'd have to do something about a picture.

If Buzz balked at showing me around, that would indicate something, too.

In a queer duplication both the Steebs gave me their work phone numbers and business cards. Each seemed to be putting forth a cryptic plea for me to contact him or her first.

They worked at a warehouse and office business complex for America's Carpets off Airport Way near the Rainier Brewery. They owned the complex, along with thirty-five other carpet stores and warehouses scattered across the Northwest.

When they retreated to the foyer to leave a retainer with

our receptionist, I collared Kathy. "How do you think it's going in court today?"

"You were there."

"So far not good."

"We haven't sprung our surprise on them."

Fast becoming notorious for her courtroom high jinks, Kathy would choreograph a charade this afternoon to impeach the credibility of the eyewitness to an armed robbery. Petunia "Frankie" Harris claimed that last January Kathy's client, Joseph Clements, had robbed her hole-in-the-wall grocery in Lake City and pistol-whipped her husband. Because her husband was too old and doddering to know who had cracked him, the only witness was Mrs. Harris. And Mrs. Harris swore Joe Clements was the perp.

The pitiful aspect to the whole thing was that Joe's former wife had admitted to me privately they had spent the night in question together, so Joe couldn't have been involved in the robbery. Yet Joe's ex-wife refused to testify in open court and vowed she would deny the alibi if we used it. A straight-laced, highly religious woman, she was mortified at the thought of admitting publicly she had slept with a man who was no longer legally her husband. Kathy argued with her for hours, but the woman refused to budge.

Kathy's brainstorm involved a man she'd hired to create a ruckus in the courtroom. He would be escorted out by the bailiff. Then Kathy would have a look-alike in identical clothing brought back into the courtroom by the same bailiff. We were hoping that Mrs. Harris would identify him with barely a glance and that the jury would notice the discrepancy. Judging by her past performances and what I'd gleaned from her neighbors and friends, she was a notorious exaggerator, an uninhibited liar, a woman who yakked her life away on the phone.

"Let me know how it goes. I probably won't see any more of it."

"You betcha."

A few minutes later Kathy and I were in the street, she on her way up the hill to the courthouse, me on my way across

Yesler to Jenny's deli. Potato salad and a turkey cranberry sandwich.

"They're a nice couple," Kathy said. "They followed me over when I left Leech, Bemis, and Ott. I don't know anything about their boys except that Faith always had a cute story about one or the other."

"And Dudley?"

"You know men have a harder time forgiving kids for their little indiscretions."

"I know my father did."

"What does a seventeen-year-old boy do out there on his own anyway?"

I thought about it for a moment. "Sleeps under bridges. Hides out in the basement of a friend's house. Moves in with an older man. Becomes a street whore."

"I hope he's all right."

"Me, too."

Kathy kissed my cheek and crossed First Avenue with the light. Under the maples a panhandler in Reeboks cadged four quarters off her. A good-looking man in a business suit tried to catch her eye and failing that, stopped and ogled the slight swing of her hips as she walked up First Avenue.

3

CLARINET MUSIC DRIFTED FROM THE REAR OF the house. Dixieland at first, smooth and uncluttered. Then a few bars snatched from classical pieces were mixed in, and I realized it was not pouring out of an expensive stereo outfit but directly from a horn.

The doorbell was frozen, the oak door ajar.

I knocked, but nobody heard me over the clarinet.

I stepped inside.

Cascadia didn't show up on my city map, but I knew where it was from my days on the force. Ten years earlier I'd been first on the scene of a rape-murder four blocks up the street. Being first on the scene like that seemed to make the whole thing a lot more real, as if it had happened to somebody you knew and loved. You could be the second one through the door, and things never were quite as personal.

The Steebs resided in a tall, immaculate white house on the west side of the street with porticoes, shutters, a balcony porch off one of the bedrooms upstairs, and an unparalleled view of Lake Washington. The house overlooked the Mercer Island Floating Bridge, the new bridge under construction, and the green hump that was Seward Park. In this neighborhood rape-murders happened about once every fifty years, if that. I wondered how often there were runaways.

Across a mile of white-nippled waters lay the expensive

beach houses of Mercer Island, the high rises of Bellevue, and the faded green rolling foothills that were a prelude to the Cascades. To the southeast loomed Mount Rainier, ominous and white and vaguely prehistoric. A rug of roly-poly clouds hugged the base of the mountain.

This neighborhood was so influential it had forced Sea-Tac to reroute flight paths. The only uncivil noise in the exclusive and sedate Mount Baker District came during the first week of August when the hydroplanes roared up and down Lake Washington and revved their engines at the Stan Sayers pits.

Orthodontists, gynecologists, and smiling morticians resided in this tasteful, ritzy neighborhood ten minutes from downtown Seattle. What real estate brokers did not point out, though, was that as soon as you got over the hill to the west and lost the view, the area deteriorated and rentals cropped up. Because this other neighborhood was within walking distance, alley windows had iron bars on them, houses were wired against intrusion, and guard dogs slept in backyards.

It was a large house with an open main floor. Sculptures, vases, and various bric-a-brac stood on tables and secretaries. The rugs had been handmade by busy little slave fingers in India or Pakistan. Before I penetrated too far into the guts of the house, I took advantage of a lull in the music and rapped on the wall.

"Come in. Come in. Am I pretty?"

I couldn't see anybody.

"Come in. Let's get some beer."

"Huh?" I said.

"Am I pretty?"

He was a yellow and green and black parrot in a huge aviary inset with monstrous mirrors, trapezes, and colored plastic geegaws. One big black eye stared at me.

"Sonja?" The music had stopped. The second voice belonged to a teenage boy.

The bird mocked him. "Sonja?"

"Thomas Black," I muttered, but all I could see was the bird, toddling back and forth sideways on a perch, cocking his head and eyeballing me. "Your parents hired me to find your brother."

When he came around the corner, clarinet in hand, he was smaller and more frightened than I would have guessed. He licked around his mouth nervously, dampening a downy black mustache that had sprouted on his upper lip. Except for his hair color, he did not resemble the dog-eared fourth-grade snapshot of his brother. He was dressed in unlaced Nike running shoes, baggy white athletic socks, yellow nylon shorts, and a paint-spattered T-shirt damp with sweat.

I stretched a hand out and found his grip limp as a glove. Unsure of himself, timid and shy, he was wary of my height and size and the general look of me. I didn't scare anyone else, but I dazzled the kids. I handed him one of my business cards, the one with the machine gun in the corner. It said, "Damsels rescued, wrongs righted, wars won." He didn't smile; but he wanted to, and when he looked up and saw my broad grin, I knew I'd broken through some sort of barrier.

"Your bird's got quite a vocabulary," I said.

"He remembers everything. We really did try to get some beer, but he told on us when Mom and Dad got home. Name is Hitler. Dad's idea of a joke." The parrot was squawking now, fanning its green and yellow wing feathers for me. "Shut up, Hitler," Buzz sighed. "It's funny what you can think is trouble. We got grounded for trying to buy beer. That was nothing compared to what Todd's done."

"What has he done?"

Buzz winced. "Being gone and all."

"Yeah. Maybe we can do something about that. By the way, you play very well."

Averting his eyes, he mumbled thanks and said, "I thought you were somebody else."

"I don't know that I've ever heard a kid your age play like that."

"You oughta hear Todd."

"He's good?"

"He wants to be a composer."

"I thought he wanted to work for the CIA."

"He figures he can do both."

"How about you?"

"Me?"

"What do you want to do?"

Buzz looked as if nobody had ever asked him the question before. "I don't know."

"I'd like to hear the two of you play together."

The house was still except for the sound of the parrot's claws on its perch.

"Your parents hired me to find your brother."

"They said they would."

"Any idea where I might start?"

"I wish I knew, Mr. Black. I hope you can find him. He's my only brother. My only family, you know. And he just took off." He halted, as if to consider the squeakiness in his voice. "Am I sounding dumb?"

"Not at all. Your folks don't seem to have a clue where he went."

"They work too hard. That's all they do. Schedules and speeding around to get to this place or that. Todd and I don't like going anywhere with them." The boy worked the keys of the clarinet, then looked nervously, almost guiltily around the room, aware that he was criticizing his parents in front of a stranger. "I guess they don't think they have enough money."

"They seem to be doing pretty well."

"More. Always more."

"People get like that. You mind answering a few questions?"

"Why would I, Mr. Black?"

"Sometimes kids run away and don't want to be found. Sometimes their brothers might want to help them."

"We have to find him."

The boy had an oddly shaped mouth, the upper teeth spaced and shaped like an upside-down fan, and like his adoptive father, he had a difficult time keeping the whole business shut. My guess was, he took more than his share of guff in school, probably not as much as his dad had taken thirty-five years ago, but enough. He was the sort of kid bullies took to.

"Do me a favor. Put your clarinet away and change your clothes. In fact, why don't you show me Todd's room? If you don't mind, I'll do some preliminary research."

"I can go like this."

"Wouldn't dream of it."

"But Todd?"

"Been missing a week. He'll still be gone in twenty minutes."

Buzz Steeb hesitated, pivoted, then trotted silently out of the room. He moved lightly, the way when you were a kid you believed Indians moved. Yet he was a clumsy-looking child, an unlikely prospect for fifth in the state in cross country, especially considering he was a sophomore. His thighs and calves didn't reveal their prowess in any obvious muscular development.

He led me up a curving flight of stairs with carpets so thick they tripped you and into an upstairs room facing the backyard and alley. I thanked him and watched him leave.

Years ago a grocery checker had asked me to locate his daughter who'd been missing three months. On a table beside the bed her mother had made up only hours after she'd disappeared, I found a long, rambling letter, still sealed, lipstick on the envelope. In their panic mom and pop had overlooked it. Their daughter had set up housekeeping with a second cousin eight years older, a fact I ascertained five minutes later by calling the operator for new listings in the town she mentioned in the note. I didn't expect that kind of luck twice, but I could try.

Elmore's room was tidier than I expected. It was as if he'd had a personal maid, though I doubted he had. Stacked next to the bedstead was a pile of running magazines, not a single torn page or dog-eared cover in the lot. An assortment of running shoes, some spiked, sat undisturbed in the closet, but there was no trace of other athletic equipment. Although there was a baby grand piano downstairs in a room off the living room, and an upright in another room on the main floor, there was a small upright against the opposite wall here. It dominated the room, and I supposed, his life.

He'd been writing his own music on blank music paper in

pencil. I was not the person to know if it was any good. Beside the door stood three tipsy stacks of sheet music, each over five feet high. I glanced through some of it. Mendelssohn. Liszt. Rachmaninoff.

Except for a hardbound copy of *The Eunuch*, a rather racy novel that had come out to some hoopla and much censoring in the late fifties, there were no books. This copy looked as if it had spent twenty years in the lending library of a tramp steamer. I remembered similarly tattered copies being passed around surreptitiously in my high school. It had been printed out of country and smuggled in. In this day and age it seemed rather tame, a curiosity reminiscent of Henry Miller or *Lady Chatterley's Lover*.

Buzz caught me looking under the bed, where I found an old railroad set. I grinned at Buzz, whose hair was wet from a shower and short enough to forgive his not passing a comb through it. He looked even paler, his spindly legs bowlegged in brown corduroy trousers. He wore a striped button-down shirt and a battered pair of last year's jogging shoes. His mother obviously bought his clothes.

"Your brother play all that music?" I asked.

"Yeah. He can sight-read through most of it. His teacher used to give him a hard time wanting him to stick with stuff and practice it, but he could play so much better than his teacher Dad got him a new one. Some woman at the U who's supposed to have been a prodigy."

"So where do you think Todd's gone? You do call him Todd?"

"Mom and Dad are the only ones who call us Elmore and Elroy. I don't know. If I knew, I'd take the bus and find him."

"He's got wheels?"

"A '53 Studebaker. Grampa left it to him in his will. Still smells new inside."

"Missing?"

"Ever since Todd left."

"Where would you look?"

"Me, Mr. Black? I'd look in Chinatown. That's the very

first place. Then I might get over to West Seattle to talk to a guy named Clay.''

"How come?" Buzz shrugged and knelt to tie a misbehaving shoelace. He had the look of a kid to whom shoelaces and zippers had always been a bugaboo. "Who's Clay?"

Buzz considered the question, avoiding my eyes when he answered. "He's an older man. There's always a bunch of kids hanging around. Girls and stuff. Todd used to go there. I went a couple of times, but I thought the old man was a creep, so I didn't go back. He was always real polite—it was almost creepy he was so polite, you know, like he had dead people in the walls—but it seemed like he was hitting on all these young chicks with his eyes, you know? And he was always telling them they could stay later if their ride was going, that he'd take them home on his motorcycle. I didn't trust him. Neither did Sonja.''

It was the name he'd called out when I knocked. "Who's Sonja?"

Clearly Buzz Steeb had strayed into territory he'd rather not have. "Todd's old girl friend.''

The boy left the room before I could pursue it.

I followed but didn't ask any more questions. He locked up and, at my suggestion, left a note for his mother, then told Hitler to shut up. A surly edge that hadn't been there before cracked his tenor voice, a man's voice that didn't seem natural coming from a boy. As we went out the front door, Hitler screeched, "Let's get some bras. Let's get us some bras.'' Buzz turned pink.

I thought he might volunteer more information about why we were going to Chinatown. He didn't. When we descended the steep concrete steps through his father's rockery to the streets where I'd parked my Ford, he said, "You're kidding? You drive a pickup truck? I've never ridden in a pickup. Can you believe that? Nobody we know owns one.''

"Much better for detectives," I said. "You're high up. Can see more. You can park in truck only zones, and it's got extra fuel tanks. I can drive to Tibet and back on one fill-up. When I knock out bad guys, I can stack 'em up in the bed like cordwood.''

"Neat."

Buzz had picked up a high-intensity flashlight from a utility closet in the kitchen, but I didn't bother to ask him what it was for.

He grinned. "How many crooks could you get back there?"

"Oh, about a hundred."

Two blocks from his house we passed a group of teenagers, some of whom peered into the cab of my truck with the studied insolence of youth. They hadn't been in jail yet and they hadn't lost a job or failed at anything important. They were still young enough and impotent enough to think it was desirable to be bad. Buzz stared ahead stolidly.

"You and Todd ever have any trouble around here?"

"Todd never does. He'll take on anybody. You can hit Todd in the face with a two-by-four, and he doesn't notice. When I'm with him, I'm okay."

"What about when you're not with him?"

"I'm careful."

4

EXITING THE NEIGHBORHOOD, WE PASSED
white-columned houses, grassy medians, sixty-foot maples,
and birches whose leaves fluttered in a light breeze and
looked like schools of small fish.

Mount Rainier Drive took us to McClellan, and then we
groped our way through traffic on a dingy Rainier Avenue
with its trucks and buses. Dearborn was like a pig trough at
feeding time, the air chalky with fine grit from bulldozers
and dump trucks. Seattle was one patch job after another.

Loud car radios pestered us and deafened their owners.
The sun was slowly heading west toward a hedge of fluffy
cumulus. As I squinted beyond the laser refractions of on-
coming traffic, I slipped on my state trooper sunglasses from
the dash.

The state was redesigning Interstate 90, adding a third
bridge to Lake Washington. Orange road signs punctuated
our frustration. Trapped behind me in the construction grid-
lock, a man in a Mitsubishi flipped me off over some imagined trespass. After a moment Buzz coughed and said, "He
gave you the bird, man."

I pulled open my jacket. "See me bleeding?"

"No." I liked the way he said it, playing the goofy, gee-
whiz kid to my Mr. Wizard.

"Tell me when I'm bleeding."

"What if he stops and tries to pull your door open, or something?"

"I got enough trouble without playing what if."

"Is that your philosophy?"

"Sometimes I pop my cork."

"Dad almost never pops his cork."

"Good for him."

"Not even when—" But Buzz stopped himself and gave me a sideways look I pretended not to see. He'd known me only twenty minutes. He had a right to be distrustful.

On Dearborn we headed west, directly toward the Kingdome, passed under the freeway viaducts, then turned north on quiet Maynard Avenue.

Every city of any size sports a Chinatown. Seattle's sprawled five or six blocks in either direction in a relatively flat tract between the freeway and the Kingdome. With its wide streets, seedy buildings, and permanent double parking, it was the only section of Seattle that reminded me of New York.

Run-down and foreign enough to impress the tourists, it didn't enchant too many locals. Instead, it had become a haven for grifters, drugged-out street walkers, dealers, and drunks who catnapped on park benches and peed into planters.

As we drove, Buzz sat very still, the way a child who's never allowed to get dirty sits. Only in his case it didn't seem to be the result of repression but rather a mood that suited his nature.

"You been a detective long?" he asked.

"Not that long. Cop for ten years. For Seattle. I liked it, liked it a lot, was planning to be chief; but I shot somebody in the line of duty, and it more or less mutilated my mental outlook."

"Did you kill 'em?"

"A kid about your age. Drilled him in the eye. He lived almost all night afterward. So now I get a pension for a bad knee, but the doctors know what it's really for."

"I read where you get over stuff like that."

"I read that, too."

"You killed anybody beside him?"

"Depends on how you define 'kill.' If I hadn't been in their vicinity, there'd be a few more people looking for parking spots."

"How many?"

"It's not something to brag about, Buzz."

He rubbed a tiny smudge off the window with his pale thumb. "Just wondering."

"Somebody dies at your hands, it makes you sick for a very long time. It doesn't make you sick, you'd better go someplace and scrub."

Buzz looked me over carefully. I didn't turn my head, but I could visualize his open mouth and separated teeth. "Sounds like something from a book."

"The truth usually sounds like something from a book."

He waited several minutes. "So how many are dead because you were there?"

"More than two. Less than ten. I'm including a guy I arrested who got hung by the state and another who got stabbed in the King County Jail. How's that grab you?"

"Sounds like a lot."

"It piles up when you've got my kind of luck."

"You carry a gun?"

"Rarely."

"Got a gun now?"

"Am I going to need one?"

"I don't see why."

"I have a couple. Not with me."

"I'd like to know how to shoot a gun."

"If it's a case that's going to require a gun, I turn the client down. Right now, I do most of my work for a lawyer in Pioneer Square named Kathy Birchfield, your folks' lawyer. That's how we got hooked up."

"So what sort of investigation do you do?"

"Mostly I look for people or try to discredit witnesses. Some money gets left to Joe Blow, but nobody can remember where Joe Blow moved to. Somebody runs away. I find 'em. A guy steals his company blind and disappears. Call Thomas Black. I like it because I'm on my own. I can use my head. I can work all night and sleep all day or vice versa. And it's me. I win, I take the credit. I don't win, I take that rap, too.''

"Ever get any weird cases?''

"Last Christmas a woman came in and claimed her husband's dog wouldn't stay out of the taverns. Lived in a small town north of here. Every drunk in town fed the mutt at these taverns. So fat he could hardly walk. They were constantly getting calls at two in the morning to come and pry him out of some doorway. She finally had him put to sleep. The husband retaliated by having her cat gassed. She asked me to sink her husband's Seville in the Snohomish River.''

"Did you do it?''

"I wanted to, but I was cleaning out my sock drawer that day.''

"You ever beat anybody up?''

"Had a woman last summer wanted me to tie her boyfriend down and yank out his teeth with rusty pliers. I gave her my dentist's number.''

"How much would you charge to break somebody's legs?''

I glanced over at him. He was as still as ever. "How much you got?''

"Six hundred dollars in savings bonds.''

"You serious?''

He nodded and gulped, but his mouth was still dry.

"Who?''

"A man.''

"I could put you in touch with somebody, but I won't.''

Buzz shrugged. Over the tops of my three-dollar sunglasses I peered at him. He was chewing the cud of an idea, had been since I met him. I cruised Chinatown, and we both looked out the windows, me for a '53 Studebaker, Buzz for his brother.

Parking on the street on Seventh in front of the China Gate, I switched the engine off and looked across the blue bench seat at the boy. When and if I had a son, I hoped he would be a little better put together, yet I felt affection for Buzz and a pang of guilt for my mental'critique. I didn't see how he could possibly dam up enough hatred to want somebody's legs broken. "Your parents mentioned suicide."

"Huh?"

"They said Todd might be thinking of killing himself." The younger brother's thick eyebrows lowered into a scowl. "They've never talked to you about it?"

"Nobody's ever talked about it. All we ever talked about was Uncle Jan. He went off the top of the old Milwaukee Hotel right up the street here. Landed on his head. They said his skull exploded like a mush melon. Does that happen? Six years ago. Jeez, I was just a kid. It seems like about a hundred years have passed, except I can still remember what Uncle Jan smelled like. After-shave and Jujyfruits. He was always popping Jujyfruits. The whole family kept it secret, you know, as if Todd and I would turn into albinos or something if we found out."

"Uncle Jan was your mom's brother? He had a reason to kill himself?"

"Nobody knows." The boy's voice grew soft and tentative. "Do heads explode like that?"

"A couple of the ones I've seen did. Don't worry. Dead is dead. It doesn't matter what happens to the body. I'm sorry you lost your uncle, though. It's tough. Sometimes it takes years to get over a suicide in a family. Sometimes you never get over it."

We got out and I fed the meter on Seventh and we walked. King Street was the spine of Chinatown, and we spiraled in on it, looping up Sixth, Seventh, Maynard Avenue, threading through all the alleys in between: Canton Alley; Maynard Alley. We saw the Tai Tung, the Hotel Alps, Liem's, the Ying Hei restaurant, Kong Yick Investments, and doorways with names over them like the Soo Yuen Benevolent Association. When he spotted the Golden Wheel Association on Weller, the third such association in a few minutes, Buzz asked me about it.

"Gambling clubs," I said. "All Chinese. Private membership. They don't open up usually until the middle of the afternoon, but then they're open all night. Most of them don't even have signs, just doors.''

Buzz shied away from a couple of wine-guzzling bums in a doorway. One of them spoke to him, ''Hey, pretty boy. You a pretty boy.''

I said, ''Not as pretty as you two buzzards,'' and Buzz laughed explosively. We spent a few minutes looking at fish and caged birds in Liem's pet shop in the alley next door to the closed-down gambling den where the Wah Mee Massacre had taken place. Buzz bought a toy for his parrot, Hitler, and put it in his pocket.

No Studebaker. No brother. We ambled along, chatted, watched faces in the crowd. I brought out the list of Todd's friends his mother had given me.

''Rankin?'' said Buzz. ''Where does she get that? Todd hasn't seen Chad Rankin in two years.''

''So who might he be in touch with?''

''I don't know. That's what bothers me. I think I'm the best friend he has. I can't think of anyone else.'' But he was lying. Even as he said it, he remembered somebody he didn't want me to know about. He wasn't the kind of kid I wanted to push around or hoodwink, so I left him his secrets.

At the park I pointed out an undercover cop flirting with a good-looking Chinese woman in turquoise. Later we watched a drug buy. We saw a man with a ponytail in a '64 Chevrolet station wagon peddle an overripe blond woman who had a face so pink it looked as if it had just been slapped. It probably had. He finally sold her to a desiccated Chinaman who was a hundred if he was a day. They went off arm in arm, a couple of twenty-dollar lovebirds, to see what rottenness they could swap. I showed Buzz how to spot shoplifters, and five minutes later he spotted one. We were doing everything but finding his brother.

When we'd made a complete and fruitless circuit of the area, I took him into the Mon Hei Chinese bakery on King and bought hombows. After we'd downed the meat pastries, Buzz said in his doleful deadpan, ''I keep having this horrible feeling somebody is going to come up

to me and say, 'Good news and bad news, kid. The bad
news is your brother's been hacked to pieces by madmen.
The good news is *Star* magazine wants to interview you
and they're paying ten bucks.''

I laughed, thinking the kid had more juice in him than
I'd given him credit for. He took me up King on the south
side of the street. Between Seventh and Maynard he
stopped, gazed across the street, and got glassy-eyed.

Between Seventh and the alley the block was one long
building, four stories tall but with half a dozen separate entrances and shops on the ground level. Conceivably you could
enter any shop and come out in a different one on the block.
Nearly everything above street level except a martial arts
parlor was vacant. Bums crept into the buildings in winter to
keep warm and snuggle up to dead pigeons.

On the southeast corner stood the Silver Dragon, smelling
like a dirty dishrag steeped in hot water. Except for the King
Café up the street it was the only restaurant I could think of
in the vicinity that was not on street level. It took up the
corner of the block on the second story.

Adjoining the Silver Dragon and taking up the rest of the
upper stories was a boarded-up hotel, paint faded, bricks
weathered, windows empty.

The Milwaukee. A faded sign on the side of the building
said ROOMS—50C AND 35C.

''That where your uncle did it?'' I asked.

He nodded and gestured at a boarded-up door under the
hotel's rooms. ''Uncle Jan used to work there. Before he got
lucky and founded America's Carpets with Dad. It was called
McCline's Towing. He drove a truck.''

The pale, chipped sign was still legible. It must have been
the only white business on the block. Even today it would
be the only white business on the block.

Buzz said, ''The offices were here. The yard they used for
trucks and wrecked cars is back on Jackson. Part of the freeway now.''

He held up the flashlight. I had a sawed-off crowbar
stashed inside my jacket. Chinatown had a lot of locked

doors and vacant buildings, and I'd had an inkling I was going to need it.

We jogged across the street.

Buzz knew the routine the way he knew where to sit at the dinner table. We traipsed upstairs into the Silver Dragon. Before we could sneak through the dim place, a Chinese woman in a yellow-gold cheongsam seated us in the nearly empty restaurant. Buzz darted a guilty look at her yellow-tan legs through the slit in her dress.

As soon as she turned her back on us, Buzz led me to the emergency exit in the southwest corner of the dining room. The exit led to a dirty stairwell, the steps unpainted, the building thick with a veil of must and dry rot. We had entered the interior stairwell of the vacant Milwaukee Hotel. If we were to descend the stairs, we would come out on the street.

I let the door settle quietly back into its niche. You could almost smell the deodorant on the ghosts. Workmen had blocked access to the upper stories with a jury-rigged plywood door across the stairway, but the hasp pulled out of the wood as if it had been violated many times before.

The boy took me up two flights and down a hallway lined with doors to rooms that probably hadn't been used since before he was born, then down another flight of creaky wooden stairs. The joint was a maze, yet everything was cleaner and in better shape than I had expected. Most of the room doors were open, as were the curtains. A wash of filtered sunlight illumined our path.

"Todd? Todd?" called out the little brother.

His feeble voice made it spookier and sadder and potentially more dangerous than if I'd been alone, but I couldn't bring myself to silence him. It was the sort of place in which you expected to find a dead man in a closet. A dead boy hanging by his belt in a doorway.

Spider webs dropped across my face like drifting cellophane. I batted at them. Either one of us could have fallen through a rotted floor or through a hole scorched by some dehorn's campfire.

We went down another set of stairs and then another. In

the second stairwell we saw evidence of someone's bivouac, but it was old and snowy with dust. A filthy newspaper on the floor was two years out of date. A mummified rat lay in the corner on his back, feet stabbing the air.

Some of the rooms had sticks of furniture. At the end of each hall were a cubicle with a bathtub and a larger room that housed three tiny commodes in stalls.

We wormed our way through passage after passage to the ground floor, where I peeped out onto the sidewalk through a window that had been blacked out but on which somebody had scraped spy holes.

Outside, I could hear a couple of Caucasian workmen arguing over who had the dirtier pair of hands and thus had been working harder. A Yellow Cab prowled the middle of King Street. In her brown work uniform a red-haired delivery-woman with big hips wheeled a hand truck toward us, then disappeared into a shop next door. I heard the sweet tinkle of the doorbell.

The Steeb boy led me through an open door with broken hinges.

"This was it. McCline's Towing. Uncle Jan worked here twenty-eight years ago. That was his desk in the corner."

"You know a lot, Buzz."

"We found some of his stuff. And he carved his initials in the desk."

"And then he killed himself six years ago?"

"Top floor."

"How old was he when he died?"

"Fifty, I guess."

Somebody had been here more recently than the campers in the stairwell. My less than expert guess was they'd been here during the past few days. The patina of dust on the floor had been scuffed. A desk had been cleared, the drawers gaping like broken piano keys. I pulled one of them open. It was cluttered with pamphlets and unused postcards from the 1962 Seattle world's fair. Pages curled, a 1959 phone book lay in the bottom drawer, along with an empty, capless fifth of scotch. Under the desk sat a six-pack of old Coke bottles.

"This leads to the basement," said Buzz, pulling open a door I'd thought belonged to a closet. "There's some stuff down there." He vanished through it.

5

I TOOK TWO STEPS AND CONKED MY FOREHEAD on a low beam.

The basement was ten times the size I'd guessed it would be, extending sixty feet end to end and about thirty feet across. Various rusted machines stood in disarray. Somebody had stacked about a hundred used car tires neatly against one wall. There were packing crates with nothing in them. The only machine I knew how to use was a roller ramp for loading merchandise down through the grates on the sidewalk and trundling it into the depths of the basement. Another apparatus, a mechanical ramp to pack the goods upstairs and into the shops, had been installed in a stairway. The place had been a beehive.

There were rooms off rooms, and in one at the far end of the basement, I heard gibberish wafting through a thin partition. Voices from inside the wall. "Elves," I whispered, and Buzz tucked his chin in and made a funny face.

Using the sawed-off crowbar, I quietly forced a chink in the partition.

A shaft of light tweezed through the wall, along with a puff of ancient black dust that choked me. I took a gander and let Buzz look. Oblivious of roaches on the walls, six elderly Chinese men were hunched around shabby tables gambling at cutthroat Pai Gow and 13-card poker.

They talked and laughed and, with shaky, wrinkled hands, manipulated painted rectangles that looked like white candy the shape of dominos. It was one of the many private gambling clubs in the area, a benevolent society of tattered old Chinese gentlemen in dowdy clothes who tottered up the sidewalks, stooping for nickels in the gutters while carrying two and three thousand dollars in their pockets. Nobody was addicted to gambling like the Chinese.

Buzz whispered against the sursurrus of their dialect, "They say there're secret passages in these basements."

"From Prohibition," I said. "And later they were used in gambling. If they got raided or robbed, the patrons wanted to be able to scoot underground to another address. The cops never have been able to crack Chinatown. Nobody in this area will talk to whites. That's why they had to set up a task force after the Wah Mee Massacre."

"Wah Mee?"

I'd forgotten how young Buzz was. He couldn't have been reading the papers at eight or nine. "Two Asian punks broke into a gambling club down here, tied everyone up, collected their money, and then proceeded to plant a bullet into each victim's brain. Twelve, thirteen men. One of them lived and eventually fingered the killers."

Buzz shuddered. "The older I get, the worse things look."

"Don't let it get you down. Plenty of things get better. Supposedly all these passages were sealed off long ago."

"Todd and I found one that wasn't. I'll show you." He led me across the room, slashing at the darkness and the cobwebs with his high-intensity flashlight.

"You and Todd spend much time in this place?"

"Lately we did. That's why I thought he might be around. Uncle Jan came here the night he died. It was like two o'clock in the morning. We were wondering what he was doing."

"You think he was visiting the offices where he used to work?"

"We know he was. The police said so."

"They find alcohol in his bloodstream? Or anything?"

"As far as we know, no. But people don't always tell the

truth to a kid—if you know what I mean.'' The boy's lip curled into a sneer of sarcasm and self-doubt.

"You don't believe he killed himself?"

Buzz Steeb didn't want to answer me but finally said, "Uncle Jan loved us. And we loved him."

It was there all right. In a small room filled with broken-down tables. He pushed a certain way on a corner of the wall, and an opening appeared, four feet across.

After we'd scuttled through the crawl space, we found another section of basement on the same level. We were gradually heading west, but my guess was we had a lot of basements to crawl through before we got to the end of this half of the block at Maynard Alley. We spent ten minutes exploring a curious setup: five tiny cubicles, each with a porcelain cleaning bowl on a stand and a single bed. They were old beds with old springs rusted stiff as bones. The mattresses were missing. In one room one of the beds had what looked like attachments for manacles at each of the four corners.

"We thought this was spook city," said Buzz. "Like white slavery or something worse. Maybe an old opium den."

A calendar on the wall was in Chinese. I couldn't get a date off it, but the place obviously hadn't been used in thirty years. "How far have you two been inside this block?"

"This is it for me. Todd comes down here by himself. He doesn't even have to go through the restaurant anymore. He's got other ways to get in. He told me he found secret passages from old gambling parlors, but I never got to see them."

"He tell you where they were?"

"I didn't pay much attention. Someplace you wouldn't suspect. I remember that."

An hour later, combing the hotel rooms again floor by floor, we zeroed in on Todd's temporary digs upstairs. The reason we hadn't seen them before was that he had nailed the doors shut from inside and exited through a window to another room.

It was one of those strange places with a three-story air shaft in the center of the building. It let out to the sky but was ringed completely by the hotel so that it rained on a roof on the first floor, but all around it were the walls of the hotel. A couple of clotheslines were still stretched across the canyon, the pulleys rusted solid. You could look into the windows of the rooms across the way, where the windows were either broken or patched with cockeyed blinds. A wooden window box across the way incarcerated grass, weeds, moss, and a vacant bird nest.

Todd's campsite was on the third floor. He had laid out a sleeping bag, a small camp lantern, a portable radio, a metal detector, and some tools in a cubbyhole of a room. A pick. Shovel. Three or four iron bars of various lengths. A hammer and a bag of nails. He had one book, *The Eunuch* again, this copy in paperback. That was it. No address books. No notes. If he ate here, there were no crumbs or wrappers littering the floor. Then again, his room at home had been immaculate except for the tools with which he had fine-tuned his days—running shoes and sheet music.

It was impossible to tell when he'd last been in the room. Maybe a week. Maybe two minutes.

The Milwaukee Hotel. Room 310. Just Elmore "Todd" Steeb and some cockroaches and an old oak dresser with nothing in the drawers and an empty metal blue and white tin of Jacob & Co.'s extra-light cream crackers that must have been as old as I was. The floor had been swept recently, was spotless.

"This is weird," said Buzz. "I mean, my own brother, and I'm tracking him down. Why would he stay in a place like this?"

"Nobody's even given me a good reason why he ran away. Except that he was supposed to have had some sort of beef with your father. It doesn't bother me. He ran away. Kids do it for all sorts of reasons."

"But what is he doing here?"

"I thought you'd tell me."

Back on the street the sunlight hurt our eyes. We went out the Silver Dragon emergency exit on the street level, and I doctored the door with tape in case I needed to get back in.

Buzz and I fed the meter again, browsed through an herb shop, a couple of Chinese groceries where I bought us sodas, then walked to the Hing Hay Park on King and Maynard and waited for Todd to pass by. We asked bums and shopkeepers about Todd, but people either didn't speak English or didn't know anything. It didn't help my cause that I didn't have a photo to pass around. We dallied in the park for an hour and fifteen minutes, Buzz feeding pigeons from a sack of day-old bread we'd gotten at the bakery. I used a pay phone on the street and dialed Kathy's office.

"How'd the case go?"

"Thomas?"

"This call's costing me a quarter, so make every word count."

"Thomas. Clements got off. Mrs. Harris retold what everyone in the courtroom had seen, and she got it so wrong it was laughable. Then, of course, she identified our ringer when the bailiff came in with him. Mrs. Harris already has another perpetrator picked out, but now she'll never convince the prosecutors. It's too bad because whoever really slugged her husband is going to skate."

"Dinner, sweetcakes?"

"You do love me."

"I'm in Chinatown. How about the Kau Kau? I need to sit by the window. The kid's been squatting in a boarded-up hotel down here. We found his stuff."

"Who's we?"

"Me and the little brother, Elroy."

"Buzz, if I remember what his mother called him. Fast work. I knew you'd come through. Hell, you found a cat that had been lost three years."

"I knew that was going to come up today."

"Well, squeeeeeeze me," said Kathy, dropping into her high-pitched gun moll's voice.

"Five o'clock? The Kau Kau? I'll walk over and reserve a table next to the window."

"What if something comes up between now and then? What if you find Todd?"

"We'll invite him."

"What about Tuesdays?"

"What about them?"

"You know what I'm talking about."

"Tuesdays is taken care of."

"So. The kid. What have you got?"

"I've got where he's staying. I should be able to stake it out and have him tonight."

"Why Chinatown? Runaways don't usually turn up there."

"The kid brother and I have been asking that same question. There's a ton of vacant real estate around. We walked through maybe sixty vacant rooms in the Milwaukee. Plenty of places to roll out a sleeping bag. But I think there's something more. His uncle died here six years ago. He bivouacked in the building where it happened."

"The uncle who committed suicide?"

"Yeah."

"Maybe this is more than just a simple runaway."

"Maybe."

"Be there at five, big guy. Promise you'll show this time? You stood me up last week."

"I was tailing that guy in your PI suit. I'll be here tonight. Cross my heart."

"I thought it was mine you were always talking about crossing."

"I'll cross yours when I get to it."

"Promises, promises, always with the promises."

"Adios, Pancho."

6

THOUGH IT WAS AS UNPRETENTIOUS AS A BOWL of rice, the Kau Kau had some of the best food in town. Besides that, it was the only restaurant on King that had tables next to the windows. It was on the north side of King, the same as the Milwaukee, just west of Maynard Alley, where all the possible back entrances of the Milwaukee Hotel were. It wasn't the best vantage point, but there was a reasonable chance we would see Todd if he headed for the Milwaukee. The Silver Dragon exit was a few doors to the east.

When Buzz spotted Katherine Birchfield sashaying through the door, I thought he was going to swallow his tongue. She wore a metallic blue body suit that had erratic stripes of vibrant colors swirling through it, a beige knit sweater knotted loosely around her neck, aerobic shoes. Her long, nearly black hair was tied in a flouncing ponytail. Her taut midriff was showing, and Buzz couldn't look away from it at first. I'd seen it before. I perused the menu. She toted a satchelful of clothing and papers from work. The skintight suit didn't leave much to the imagination, which was the way Kathy liked it. Always the bull's-eye on the target.

Though she was of less than average height for a woman, Kathy's legs were so long they made her look taller. She had studied dance, and her figure was the result of years of workouts. Slim. Lithe. Small-breasted. She had that sort of sexy,

38

perky personality that somehow managed to sucker every man at the party into thinking he was in love with her.

Her habit was to introduce me as *her* detective because she knew it annoyed me, made me sound like her pet poodle, and because I had yet to think up a reply that was anything but inept. Verbally abusing me sent Kathy into gales of laughter. You don't mind a thing like that when she's a lawyer who looks like a professional showgirl and doesn't take herself seriously in the least. Leastways I didn't.

It took her three minutes to unravel Buzz's nervousness. Buzz was confused and enthralled at the same time. I watched him blink and gulp after Kathy had inadvertently used a swear word. When you're fourteen, going on fifteen, sometimes it takes a minute or two to catch up to the real world.

Our waiter was a tallish Chinese woman, and after she left, Kathy leaned so close I could feel her hot cheek against mine, and she whispered, "Got crumbs on your face." Buzz watched in undisguised awe. When I was just about his age, I'd been exposed to a woman about half as entrancing, so I could almost gauge Kathy's effect on the boy.

"So," she said, focusing on Buzz, "let's hear all about your cross-country running. I understand you got fifth in the state."

The boy glanced at me and then at Kathy, who was beaming at him, and blurted out the details of the championship race. In the mornings before school, Todd and Buzz trained together on Lake Washington Boulevard. When the championship meet came last winter, Todd copped first place. Todd could beat anybody, anywhere, anytime. Elroy Steeb bragged about his older brother the way small children bragged about their fathers, and I caught a glimpse of how much Todd's escapade must have wounded him.

"Why'd Todd quit the team?" I asked, keeping an eye on the street outside.

He wasn't a fidgety kid, but he fidgeted now. "You know about that?"

"Your parents told me."

"You see, Coach Blankenship makes a big thing every year of watching the first tryouts and predicting who is going to be hot and who is not. In fact, he writes it all down, and at the end of the season he shows it to everyone. Anyway, he predicted Todd would quit after a week. And if he didn't quit, he said he'd be last in everything. Todd just got better and better, and Coach couldn't figure it out. He didn't particularly like it either. Todd has his own way of training, too. I guess it kind of undermined Coach's authority.''

''So he quit because of the coach?''

''Todd had a lot of pressure on him. All sorts. I don't think it was really much to do with Blankenship. He's kind of gruff, but Todd really antagonized him one day. He shoved Todd, and Todd said he didn't need this and quit. Things were just getting to him. I quit, too.''

''Why you?'' Kathy asked.

''Todd's done things for me. I owe him. He told me not to, but I think secretly he was glad.''

''What kind of kid is your brother?'' I asked. ''Really. What kind?''

The meal came, and while the waitress served it, Buzz sat silently. When we were alone again, he looked at the shrimp-fried rice and said, ''Todd's old girl friend said this once, and I never forgot it. It had something to do with—You know how high school is? One of my teachers told us everything was the same when she was in school, so I guess you'll know. It's kind of a minicity, you know? A microcosm, she called it.

''There's a pecking order. Who's popular and who's not. There are those who are in. There are those who want to be in. And there are those who pretend they don't care but who really want to be in. And then there's Todd. He's not in, he doesn't want to be in, he doesn't care if you're in, he doesn't give a damn who is or isn't, and everybody knows it. He short-circuited the system. Not very many kids do that.''

I couldn't help recalling how worried Todd's mother was over the possibility of suicide.

''Where do you fit?'' asked Kathy. ''In? Want to be in? Don't give a hoot?''

Her sudden, caring scrutiny and blue-violet eyes embarrassed and snake-charmed him at the same time. ''Me?'' His

chagrin turned a smile into an unintentional smirk. "I'm just
a sophomore."

He thought about my earlier question. "Todd's running
became a pain, ya know. Because he did it but he didn't live
for it. He lived for his music, that he lived for. I mean, for a
while there it was all he thought about. He'd get home from
school and start practicing, take a short break for dinner, and
play late into the night. Every night. The running was like
to blow off steam or something from all the sitting. In the
summer, when he was younger and had all day, he'd practice
for six or seven hours every day, for weeks on end. He had
trouble with the joints in his fingers from all the playing. Dad
thinks it's crazy. Dad has a tin ear."

We ate, and Kathy talked about a complex legal case she'd
been reading about in the *Wall Street Journal* that was going
to affect something she was handling for a firm in Spokane.
Her office was new, and she didn't have many cases, so she
nursed each. We polished off the fortune cookies and hogged
the table long after we should have released it. The more I
saw of Buzz, the more I liked him. He was ingenuous to a
fault. Sweet.

It was almost seven-thirty, and we all were so full of tea
we were ready to burst when I looked out on the shadowed
street. "That your brother?"

After periscoping his head up to glance over a parked car
outside the window, Buzz knocked his chair over to run out
of the room and around the partition, then out through the
front door. I started to follow, called over my shoulder, "It's
on you tonight, Kathy. I'll be back." But she was behind
me, pulling.

"Just stay here a minute, bub," she said.

"What'sa matter? Broke?"

"Just leave them alone a few minutes."

She was right. She got her bag, and I paid the bill and
stood in the tiny glassed-in foyer of the Kau Kau and watched
the two boys converse animatedly sixty yards up the street.
They were a matched set.

Todd was taller than Buzz and much better glued together,
though not any heavier. He didn't exhibit the clumsiness Buzz

did, didn't look quite so disjointed. Perhaps Buzz would out-
grow it in two years. Todd wore a leather flight jacket, which
must have been hot in this weather, baggy khaki trousers,
and the obligatory running shoes.

Todd looked jumpy, peering up the shadowed street toward the Kau Kau. Calmer, Buzz pointed toward us and said
something. Todd shook his head, but Buzz persisted. Just
from the body language, it was easy to see how close the
boys were.

I said, "He's going to run."

"Baloney," said Kathy. "How do you tell a thing like
that?"

"He's spooky. Just look at him."

"Maybe if I go out myself. Alone. Nobody's going to run
from a woman. Especially this woman."

"Don't flatter yourself."

"What'll we bet?"

"You have to ride twenty miles on a bike with me if you
lose."

"Fine, buster. And you have to spend a session in my
aerobics class."

She hadn't even cleared the doorway when Todd began
jogging east on King, away from us, and away from his
brother, who raised his hands in a gesture of supplication,
shouting so that we could hear his voice but not his words.
The older brother cast a single glance over his shoulder and
continued. I was past Kathy before she could call me bub.

I went up King and hooked a left at Seventh, heading
north. Todd was only a quarter of a block in front. When he
saw me, he turned on the afterburners, reached Jackson, and
headed toward downtown, coattail flapping. The boy could
run. So could his younger brother, who came sailing past
me, gasping, "Mr. Black, I can't talk any sense into him."

Half a block west on Jackson, Todd took a shortcut through
Maynard Alley, presumably to tuck into a doorway or maybe
sneak into the Milwaukee through one of his secret entrances. I doubted Buzz had had time to tell him we'd found
his hideout. He was completing a circle.

Buzz on his heels, he hit King Street at the spot where I'd started and headed west, passing the Kau Kau. Passing Kathy.

In the alley I'd seen a small object in silhouette tumbling out of Todd Steeb's jacket pocket. I lost a moment or two picking it up. I couldn't run anywhere near as fast as either of them or zigzag in and out of the pedestrians the way they could. I was hoping they'd be impeded by traffic or a cop would stick his foot out or maybe Todd would think better of his flight.

They flew toward the King Street train station, north along Fourth Avenue, where there were no more tall buildings along the sidewalks, and then, when three motorcycle policemen scrutinized them, they were forced to slow the pace. I could see Buzz, who had apprehended his brother, trying to talk to him. I kept running and came within a block.

Todd jogged across Fourth Avenue, crossed Jackson again, and went down the underpass to the railroad tracks. I wasn't getting any closer, but when the two of them disappeared into the tunnel I knew it was over. The train tunnel ran under downtown Seattle. More than a mile long. No way was I going to catch either of them in the darkness.

Stopping at the mouth of the tunnel, I called out, but the only reply I got was the sound of footfalls. The sounds grew fainter and fainter.

Heaving, I placed my hands on my knees and leaned over until I caught my breath. I was in excellent shape, but it had been a sorry contest. I fondled the packet that had dropped out of Todd Steeb's coat in the alley, revolving it three or four times in the light.

As near as I could tell there were a hundred bills in the packet. All hundreds. Stiff and smelling of banks and sneaky deals and somebody's secret sins. Where would a seventeen-year-old boy get ten grand? And why carry it around in his pocket?

7

PONYTAIL SWINGING, KATHY MET ME ON KING Street and walked me to my truck. "I'll tune up your ten-speed," I said.

"You three were flying." Worry lines laddered her forehead. "What's the matter?"

"I lost them."

"I could have told you that."

"The pity is, I don't think if he changed his clothes, I could recognize him up close."

After driving the pickup down to the waterfront, we waited at the other end of the tunnel on Alaskan Way, though we had no idea where they would come out. Maybe they had already gone back to Jackson Street and emerged. Then, too, if Burlington Northern had excavated any other exits, I wasn't aware of them.

"I hope a train doesn't come while they're inside," said Kathy.

Twice I got out of the truck and walked to the tunnel mouth. No boys, no trains, and no jitterbugging flashlight.

Kathy slumped low in the truck seat. "Now we've got two of them missing."

"Thanks for reminding me."

"Sorry."

"I've got a feeling Buzz'll be back. I don't think his brother wants him tramping around the city on his heels."

"He's such a nice kid," said Kathy.

"He wanted me to break somebody's legs."

"What?"

"Six hundred bucks." She had a grip on my arm, around the biceps, something she was always doing. She was a toucher. I wasn't, and it made for some interesting moments.

"Whose?"

"Whose what?" I was looking at her grip.

"Whose legs did he want broken?"

"He wouldn't say."

I thought about the request coming from a boy whose actions were so gentle he'd had to slam my truck door three times before it closed properly.

"Thomas, what on earth did you tell him?"

"Said I only worked over cripples and fat ladies."

Kathy made her lower lip swell and gave me one of her hired-killer looks. I reached out and flubbed her lip with my finger. It didn't alter her mood. After a bit I said, "Ever read *The Eunuch*?"

"One of my old boyfriends was into it. Saw the movie maybe fifteen times. He lives here in town, you know."

"Your old boyfriend?"

"The guy who wrote *The Eunuch*, dummy. They say he's weird. Sure. It was a classic. Everybody who goes to college gets their hands on a copy sooner or later."

"I found a hard-cover in Todd's room in the Mount Baker District and another copy in the Hotel Milwaukee with his sleeping bag."

"He's about the right age," said Kathy. "You read it in college?"

"Yeah. Even saw the movie. A masterpiece."

"They say it's one of the most underrated films of all time."

"They say."

We waited twenty-five minutes, then checked the other end of downtown near Chinatown. I kept playing the story line of *The Eunuch* over in my mind, trying to figure out why

Todd would be so enamored of it. It had been published by an underground press, and then the film had been shot in Spain, South America, and Mexico and clandestinely in California studios. The movie had finally gained critical acclaim in France and eventually the rest of Europe.

The story was a postapocalyptic tale of a young fighting man named Rom from the northern outskirts of civilization. Rom stumbles upon a roving band of priests. In a bloody confrontation he rescues the priests from a Bedouin gang as the gang prepares to castrate them ritually.

Taking Rom under their protection in a land alien to him, the priests discover Rom is fertile. Because of an irresponsible chemical experiment one of the developing nations let loose on civilization, the earth is rapidly losing its population, and male infertility has spread like a plague. In two hundred years the planet has gone from billions to fewer than five million, and the population is still being decimated. Of the hundreds of thousands of males left on earth, only a handful remain able to impregnate a female, a gift that makes a man a demigod in the culture. Males with the ability are pressed into the priesthood.

As the world's population dies off and is not replaced, as union after union remains barren, as disease spreads, as governments collapse because there is no longer anyone to govern, as war ravages the populace, a bizarre religion springs up, its basis rooted in conception, its sole aim being perpetuation of the species. Its primary rite: sexual intercourse. The priests are worshipped since their ejaculations are the key to the future.

In the new religion the hat trick for women is to conceive from a single coupling, and to this end the priests have become biologists unparalleled in history, though most other earth sciences have died out.

The only nonbelievers are the Bedouin tribes, who kidnap babies and pregnant females and who castrate priests when they catch them.

The priests roam the land, visiting temples. Ovulating females are brought to them each night. Priests are so scarce that an area may not receive a visit for two or three years.

During that interval no children are conceived. Even after a visit a settlement of two thousand may register a mere twenty or thirty births.

The rules of the Effnick religion are as elaborate as any in history. When a female breaks a rule, she is beheaded. Eunuchs do the judging and the axing. Only a priest can overrule them. For major infractions, like falling in love or two couplings with a virgin, priests are privately whipped. Spilling his seed or expending it on a subject who has not been passed by the genetic board may call for a priest to be publicly made into a eunuch. Afterward he may be stoned to death.

The novel was more than 1,500 pages, the movie 190 minutes. Young people, especially, seemed to respond to the bizarre plot. People had committed suicide gripping copies of the novel. School boards banned it. Preachers harangued it. Schoolboys masturbated with it.

I hadn't seen the movie in years, though it constantly played at some art house around the country or in basement rooms in universities.

Fifty minutes after I lost him, Buzz popped up on Alaskan Way in front of the aquarium, his brother nowhere in evidence. I stopped the truck, and Buzz climbed in beside Kathy.

"So?" Kathy said to Buzz.

Looking out the window, Buzz locked the door and fastened his seat belt. "So," he said, unexpectedly cloaking himself in a teenager's sarcasm.

"What happened?"

"Nothing."

"You want him back home, or what?"

"It's not that simple. He'll come back when he's ready." Buzz thought about what he'd said, ran a pale hand through his dark, cropped hair. "I dunno. Maybe . . . You'll never catch him if he doesn't want you to."

"Don't be too sure," I said. "I think he's in trouble."

"So do I, Mr. Black." Then Buzz's voice rose to a near shout. "He wouldn't tell me anything!"

"That's okay," said Kathy. "That's okay."

"But he wouldn't tell me. He always tells me. And he looks . . . wild. Like he hasn't been getting any sleep. Or . . ."

"Drugs?" I said.

"I dunno."

"Has he ever done drugs?"

"Some guys wanted him to take steroids for his running, put some muscle on him, you know. But he wouldn't. I guess we've smoked a joint or two."

"Anything else?"

"Unh-unh."

"You tell him we found his sleeping bag in the Milwaukee?"

"I guess—I guess I accidentally did. Not too smart, huh?"

"I wouldn't have caught him there tonight anyway. Look, whatever he's into, I'll help. Understand?"

"Would you really?"

"If he doesn't want to come with me, that's fine. I won't force him. He can stay on the street forever, but I'm not going to stop until I at least talk to him."

"He thought you were going to use handcuffs. I told him you weren't that kind of guy, but he didn't believe me."

"You free tomorrow, Buzz?"

"I've got school. But it's the last week. Everybody's skipping."

"Tell you what, kiddo. Kathy'll drive you home in her Triumph. And I'll see you at your place tomorrow morning around eight-thirty. Deal?"

"Deal."

"We'll check out that Clay guy you told me about."

"Yeah," he said, his throat dry. Driving home with Kathy wasn't going to hurt him a bit. In fact, he'd probably fantasize about it for years. "He told me that's where he was today."

"Clay?"

"Yeah. But he won't go back tonight. The old man was going out."

After I'd dropped them off at the lot where Kathy'd left her car, I drove to her office on First Avenue. There was a communal safe in a back room behind a coffee machine. It didn't have much in it except documents and a sack of coffee beans one of the other lawyers claimed kept it smelling legal. After counting the hundred-dollar bills, I slid the bundle into a manila envelope, licked and sealed it, marked it "Thomas Black—for the Steeb case," dated it, then tossed it inside. There were ninety-nine bills in the envelope, all hundreds, all uncirculated.

I drove back to the waterfront, keeping an eye out for a young man in a leather flight jacket, then parked in the lot at the Edgewater Inn not far from where we'd found Buzz. I walked into the first-floor lounge at the Edgewater and ordered a 7-Up from the bar, sat on a barstool, sipping from the soda for a few minutes, surveying the room, the patrons, and, through the windows, the purplish pink sunset over Elliott Bay.

A jittery man with snake eyes and a good head of hair stacked himself on the barstool next to me. He was maybe five years younger than I was but dressed as if he were eighteen. "Nice headlights," he quipped after a pair of women walked past and sat in a corner with two men. "Come here often?"

"Me?" I said. "Almost never."

"I heard it was a good place to pick up babes."

"S'pose."

"You just here by yourself, or what?"

I nodded.

"Gonna meet some friends, but I like to get to a place early and scope it out, know what I mean? If there's any gorgeous ladies around, maybe I can swoop on 'em before my friends mess up the action, know what I mean?" He leaned close and used his bouncing eyebrows for emphasis.

"Sure."

"There's a couple at the end of the bar there," he said. "Claim they're waiting for their boyfriends. Mercer Island rich bitches. How about that one over there at the table?"

"Where?"

A woman sat with her back to the room, gazing out at the purplish sky. Her tawny hair was cut short, exposing a white neck. She wore large glasses; relaxed, alone, she looked attractive and rather bookish.

"Maybe one of us should vulture in on that," said my friend, eyebrows dancing.

"Maybe one of us should." I sipped my drink, ice clinking against my teeth. I didn't move.

"Well, what's she going to do? Tell my mother?" The lounge lizard picked up his bourbon and slithered over, waggling his hips. Without an invitation he sat next to the woman in the glasses, slammed his drink on the table, and began jabbering. She didn't look away from the sunset. She said something clipped. He answered. She said something else, and he picked up his drink and trotted back to the bar, except that his walk was different now, more like a forced march. "Bitch," he said.

"What'd she say?"

"Just a bitch, 's all."

"No, what'd she say?"

"She thinks she has a right to sit alone. Hell, what does a woman come to a place like this for if she doesn't want to get picked up?"

"Maybe you should have used a more direct technique."

"Yeah," he said bitterly. "Maybe I should have boffed her one and thrown the salami to her. She'd understand that."

"I didn't realize guys like you still existed," I said. "I thought penicillin had wiped you out." I picked up my soda and walked quietly across the room to the woman in tortoiseshell glasses. I leaned over and whispered something in her ear. It didn't startle her the way I imagined it would. She didn't turn away from the window. I glanced at the man at the bar and shrugged. He scowled.

"I told your friend I was here to meet someone," she said, staring at my reflection in the glass.

"He's not my friend."

8

"HE WAS A LITTLE UNPOLISHED."

"I'll have a word with him."

"Don't ruffle your feathers on my account."

The soda was too sweet. "Okay, you talked me out of it."

I was afraid she was going to get snooty. She had the self-assurance, sometimes mistaken for iciness, not often seen in a woman alone. It automatically made her a target for the male of the species. Perhaps it was the challenge. Some guys preferred an uphill battle.

An incoming ferry captured our attention. A boisterous party of women entered the room, giggling and talking loudly.

She wasn't beautiful. In fact, if you analyzed it, she rode the fence between handsome and plain. Her skin was flawless; her features were good, teeth white and even. She was a woman who had been someplace. You might call her striking, though she could slip past you in a crowd. She crossed her legs and kicked one shoe loose, the white ridges on the arch of her foot showing.

She said, "I was waiting for the sky to get dark, and then I was heading home."

"Pity to throw away a night like this."

"You may be right."

"There'll be stars. You can smell the salt water, even in

51

here. I love the ferries at night. They look like huge space-ships.''

''They do. I've just been letting the ambience take hold of me.''

''Uh-huh.''

I watched her hazel eyes as she searched my brown ones. She said, ''You look a little dragged out.''

''Had a funny day. You have dinner yet?''

''A long time ago.''

''Me, too.''

She caressed the back of my hand with a fingertip. ''I've got all night, Thomas.''

I watched the shoe about to fall off her bare toes. ''You propositioning me, lady?''

I caught a whiff of her perfume as she took my hand, and we stood and went upstairs to a room on the third floor over-looking Elliott Bay, the Olympic Mountains, the light buoy at Duwamish Head. We talked. I took a shower. We made love. We talked some more. We talked about stupid things: a bill before Congress, a fender bender she'd been involved in three weeks earlier; the price of avocados. When you saw a woman only once a week, it was like the first time every time. And still, we talked about stupid things. Nattering was one of the special features of our relationship.

It had been several months since Judy Banner and I first ran into each other in Borracchini's bakery. She'd come in with a group of young handicapped adults, some in wheel-chairs, some in headgear, some drooling, some gaping, some retarded. She was a caretaker at a home.

I had dropped in with a female cycling companion, in tights and heavy wool jackets and wool gloves—it had been before the weather had turned—and we waited in line to buy a package of anise Italian biscuits with the little colored chips of dried fruit embedded in them.

That day the twelve in her group were too much for her to handle. One of them looked ill, and a couple were clamoring for attention. Judy had been patient and exasperated at the same time. The other patrons were beginning to evacuate the premises as if she and her charges were escapees from an LSD nightmare.

Sans makeup, she had been clad in worn-out jeans and a knit sweater that looked as if it'd spent the winter as a doormat. She wasn't anything special. Except for her athletic body, she was rather plain.

It was her attitude that hooked me.

Awed by her patience, I tried to get eye contact, but she was too busy to pay any attention. Sometimes you can say little things with your eyes that you could never get across with words, but she wouldn't let me. It was then that I noticed the wedding band on her pale left hand.

A month later I saw her at lower Woodland Park. Kathy's softball team was battling hers, and I was gobbling hot dogs in the bleachers, cheering Kathy, razzing the other team.

She wore makeup this time and trim blue shorts with gold piping and a baseball cap, and her muscular legs were showing, but they were white because she didn't get much sun— and no wedding band. It blew me away. The whole thing. She was one of the strongest players on the team. I asked her out, and without hesitation she said no.

Half an hour later she approached me shyly and asked if the invitation was still good. She folded her arms and waited for me to reply. From the first there was a quiet electricity between us.

I suppose I was ready for sparks. I had friends, but I hadn't had a lover in ages. And I kept thinking about getting married.

It was a funny deal from the word "go," but I went with it . . . just because. And Judy went with it for reasons of her own.

The rule was I could see her any Tuesday it wasn't raining, and she wasn't going to explain, and I wasn't to ask again because my asking gave her a headache.

When the weather was bad, she simply did not show. Drizzle, rain, scattered showers: performance canceled. To set the time and place, I called her at the home on Capitol Hill near Volunteer Park. She called me only once. Knowing I was a private detective, she asked me not to sneak around and probe into her life. I didn't.

I was perilously close to being in love with her in a way that might not go away.

She worked six, seven days a week, twelve and fourteen hours a day. She worked on salary, so she got no overtime, yet she loved it, nursed the patients as if each were her own child. She called them 'My Jimmy. My Rose. My Richard.'

Judy was twenty-six. She had no children and was not living with a husband. I knew from the ring she had been married once. Probably still was. I could find out easily enough, but I had promised.

Twice now she'd shooed me out of restaurants when she recognized friends. The first time had been our first date, so I had had no illusions, yet I'd glimpsed her apartment and she was living alone.

Sometimes we'd go to a movie and then a hotel. Sometimes dinner first. Twice we went to the ACT and saw plays. Sometimes just the rented room. Always a hotel. Never her place. Never mine. Invariably she tiptoed out of the room in the wee hours, carrying her coat and car keys.

I was beat. Beside the Clements trial, I'd been up late the previous night doing interviews on a hit-and-run in which four people had gone to the hospital. I had put ads in the papers and slapped up about a thousand flyers. I thought I had the vehicle and driver located in Enumclaw.

Judy and I had never had a morning together before, and I wasn't prepared for the way she woke me. Afterward we took a shower together, and I glimpsed my hair in the mirror, jutting out in a dozen directions. Where's gravity when you need it?

As the hot spray needled our shoulders, she said, "Doesn't it occur to you sometimes that I'm using you?"

"From time to time."

"And?"

"If everybody used me like this, I'd die of terminal ecstasy."

"Be serious." She scrubbed my chest with a bar of soap.

"Yeah, it bothers me."

"And?"

"I've been playing it week by week."

"Go on."

"So far I don't mind."

"Don't you want to know more about me?"

"Not if you don't want me to know."

She gazed into my eyes for a long time, then laid her wet head against my shoulder. I hoped she wasn't saying good-bye because it was going to kill me. What she said was "I might have an entire day free later in the week."

"I'm on a case. I'm not sure how much free time I'll have."

"Call?"

"It'd take an army to stop me."

It was five to eight when I got home. In his suspenders, jeans, and Mariners cap, my grouchy neighbor, Horace, waved a gnarled hand at me and went back to weeding his hydrangeas. I'd had a dog once who'd gotten a big kick out of messing with those hydrangeas, but that had been long ago, and now the dog was in a grave under a Whiskey Mac in the back yard. It had been a bad time.

My home was in the University District off Roosevelt Way in a two-bedroom bungalow that might have been called slum housing by the Steebs but that was clean and comfortable and suited me just fine. I worked on my truck in the single detached garage. I cultivated forty-two varieties of roses in the yard, added a variety or two each spring. Since the house was close to the U, there was always somebody after the apartment in my basement.

The first thing to greet my eyes was a bouquet of roses I'd cut for Judy but hadn't had time to take to her. Then I saw the box containing the throw-out bearing I had planned to install in my '68 Ford. It had been a rushed week.

After pouring some bran into a bowl, I buried it in sliced strawberries from the backyard, filled it half full with skim milk, and went into the bedroom to change clothes.

When I went into the bathroom, I was wearing a pair of corduroy trousers and nothing else. "Shoot!" I said.

"Hey, big fella."

She was in the tub, soaking.

"What the hell are you doing?"

"Taking a bath, silly. For a detective, you're not very observant."

Masking my eyes with one hand, I said, "It's just luck that I even had my pants on."

"Good or bad luck, Cisco?"

"Why are you doing this?"

"Now wait a minute, bub. When you let me move back downstairs, you promised to put a tub in, and so far all I see is a shower that leaks."

"I thought I smelled bubble bath when I came in the back door." Brunette hair tucked up and pinned, Kathy was thoughtfully reckless about how she moved about in that glacier of bubbles. They were thinner than they should have been for this sort of hanky-panky. "Okay, sister. I'll get to that tub before the month is out. Cross my heart."

"I thought it was *my* heart—"

"Yeah, I've heard that one."

"Where have you been? As if I need to ask. How was Tuesday?"

"Fine." Schooled in the loopholes of my life, Kathy managed to keep track of my love life in a way I couldn't with hers.

"Still beautiful?"

"Jealous?"

"She's duping you, Thomas."

"You've said that before."

"I know. And I don't want to harp on it. So what were you guys doing? Besides the obvious."

"Just out on a toot."

"You? A toot?" She laughed, and it reverberated off the tile bathroom like music. "You don't even drink. Your idea of a toot is riding your bike forty miles or playing basketball with the neighborhood kids for half the afternoon."

"The Edgewater," I said, picking up my electric razor and plugging it in.

"Ooooh. Ritzy."

"Look, I'll be out of here in a jiffy."

"Take your time, mister. I've been reading this book. I had an old copy lying around." She held up *The Eunuch*, and I looked in the mirror, then away. "It's interesting."

"Clayton James," I said, reading the author's name backward in the mirror. "Think they call him Clay?"

"You're going to see a guy named Clay today, aren't you? With Buzz. I caught that last night. I came up to ask you about it, but you weren't here. I found some strawberry-rhubarb pie in the fridge. You don't mind?"

"You made it for me."

"It's quite dirty without using any of the standard slang. I don't remember its being this risqué."

Finished shaving, I splashed some cologne on in case I met some tough guys, went into the bedroom, and threw on a sport shirt, then grabbed a jacket. The morning chill hadn't lifted yet, though the sky was a pale blue. A balmy seventy or seventy-five today.

"There's something you're not telling me, bub," Kathy said, wandering out of the bathroom in a robe as I downed breakfast. She left wet tracks on the floor.

"Don't worry your pretty little head about it."

She snickered at my patronizing remark. "This Clayton James is a legend around town. You know that, don't you?"

"Yeah, I know it. See ya later."

"Same to ya."

She stroked my cheek with a damp hand as I strode out the back door. Sometimes it was disquieting to have a best friend of the opposite sex, especially one as pretty and unattached as Kathy. Lately I had been flashing back to the night last summer when Kathy saved my life. She touched me after that, too, and I had felt something for her I hadn't felt since our first meeting.

We'd been waiting at a phone booth in Kent for a call from a witness it had taken me three weeks to track down. The night was sweltering, almost airless. Half a block up the street a man began ranting and kicking out headlights on parked cars. When I got out of my truck and yelled for him to stop, he came after me in a slow jog.

From a hundred yards he hadn't looked like much, but the

closer he got, the more I thought I'd made a serious miscalculation. He was six-six, weighed an easy hundred pounds more than I did, and his eyes resembled pie plates with .22 bullet holes in the centers. One arm was bloody. Using a fist the size of a Volkswagen, he whacked me across the cheek. The blow knocked me to the ground. Warily I stood up and punched him in the solar plexus. It was like hitting a bag of sand.

"I'm going to kill you," he said, unsnapping the Buck knife case on his belt. It was empty. "I ain't got no knife," he said, "but I got this." Using his other hand, he brought a straight razor out of his rear pocket.

I ran.

He might have killed me if Kathy hadn't run over him with my truck. She hit him, then accelerated fifty feet across the parking lot with his body draped across the hood. I trotted over to see if he was dead yet.

The Ford's engine idled. Kathy had locked the doors, a tic in one cheek, her knuckles bone white on the steering wheel. She tried to smile but succeeded only in baring her teeth. Lying underneath the front of the truck, my assailant opened his eyes and spoke deliberately, so that there was no mistaking his intention. He said, "When I get up, I'm going to kill you."

I kicked him in the face. He rolled over, shook himself, looked at me, and said, "When I get up, I'm going to kill you." We repeated the quadrille until my dance card was filled.

PCP. Angel dust.

Even beaten and bloodied as he was, it took eight police fifteen minutes to get him into restraints.

His Buck knife was missing because he'd tried to cut his arm off with it, found it too dull, then buried it in a telephone pole.

Elbows on his knees, hands cupping his chin, Buzz was sitting on his front porch. He jogged down the concrete steps and clambered into my Ford. His hair was damp and frizzy from a shower.

"How you doin', kid?"

"Fine," he said, his voice soft as an August breeze.

"Clayton James, huh?"

"There's something I should have told you last night. But didn't."

I turned to him. "What's that?"

"Todd did say something. There's some money involved. He was talking like maybe a million dollars. I dunno. Maybe half a million. It's supposed to be laying around somewhere in cash."

"Is it?"

"Todd thinks so."

"So why doesn't he pick it up and get rich?"

"He says he can't find it. But his eyes? Remember I told you his eyes didn't look right and you asked me if it was drugs?"

"Yeah."

"He's scared."

"What makes you say that?"

"I remembered. His eyes look like that when he's scared, Mr. Black. It took me awhile to figure it out because with Todd it doesn't happen that often. He's real scared."

"He say anything to you about it?"

"Todd? No way, man."

9

UNABLE TO RECALL THE ADDRESS AND UN-
aware of the street names, Buzz directed me by landmarks.

We drove into West Seattle across the new Spokane Street
Bridge, where we got a good look beyond the huge orange
loading cranes on Harbor Island at the sprawl of downtown.
To the south the poisonous haze that frequently blanketed the
Duwamish Valley and its industry had been ushered away by
a frisky wind.

Isolated from the rest of the city by the Duwamish Water-
way and Elliott Bay, West Seattle had been annexed by the
city years ago. Ocean tankers and salmon fishermen in small
boats anchored between us and downtown. A tidy little place,
West Seattle had managed to keep a small-town feel about
it.

Thirty-fifth Southwest took us south along the ridge, past
the High Point housing project, up beyond the water towers,
past the highest point in the city, and down to Barton Street.
After the Christian Science church we wound downhill toward the water. A ferry chugged toward the Fauntleroy dock
below.

Buzz said, "What are you going to say when we get
there?"

"I'll think of something."

"What if he throws us out?"

"They ain't gettin' no cherry." Buzz laughed hesitantly. "How many times have you been here?"

"Two."

"What went on?"

"Nothing much. I had the feeling it all happened after I was gone. He's a creepy guy. You oughta see his wife."

"What did Todd say went on here?"

"Todd didn't say. The night I was there the old guy mostly talked, and the rest of them mostly sat around and listened, you know."

Toward the bottom of the hill we turned off on Forty-first Avenue Southwest into a quiet neighborhood of immaculate brick houses. I'd mark it on my map and come back next Christmas with Aunt Charlotte and we'd chirrup over the colored lights. Buzz pointed out a house on a corner. I took note of the address and parked my truck.

The yard was a triple lot, terraced, overlooking the sound. It was all so upper-middle-class and sedate it was hard to believe *the* Clayton James lived here. I'd pictured something garish, a Gothic mansion with creepers obscuring the windows, bougainvillaea smothering the gazebo, and a mad grounds keeper hacking at weeds with an oversize sickle.

After a long wait a man clothed in a very old, natty, and out-of-date suit answered the door. He carried a silver tray the way butlers did in the old movies, balanced on his splayed fingertips.

A small, thin-boned man, he wore a mustache that had been pared down until it looked like black whip marks. He was maybe sixty, a faded sixty from a life of abuse. He reminded me of a smaller David Niven.

"So sorry," he said, with a trace of an English accent, tidying his vest with his free hand. "Could you manage to wait a moment? I'll be right with you."

If he recognized Buzz, he gave no hint, yet he acted as if we were expected. He glided through a very ordinary house highlighted by hardwood floors, cheap prints on the walls, and furniture purchased twenty years ago. Toward the rear of the house he stopped, balanced the tray precariously in one hand, rapped at a door, said something, then entered. I couldn't see into the room.

"That him?"

"Yup," said Buzz, who giggled nervously.

Before I could get any more information, Clayton James blizted through the entryway and went into the kitchen. Ice knocked around in a tall glass as he came trundling back with orange juice in a tumbler. He took it to the room, came out, closed the door, and met me.

"Clayton James?"

"And you are?"

I handed him one of my cards—one without the machine gun. "Trying to track down this young man's older brother. His name is Elmore Steeb. Nicknamed Todd."

Slowly turning his full attention to Buzz, James said, "I'm afraid I'm at a loss. I don't believe I know your brother."

Unsure, Buzz glanced at me, then back to James. "He plays the piano."

"Hmmm," said James, fingering his mustache delicately. "*That* Todd. Won't you have a seat?" He placed us on a sofa, then dropped into an easy chair so that the window was at his back, the morning light bracketing him. I couldn't help looking out at Vashon Island when I should have been looking at his eyes. They were Komodo dragon eyes, black as tar.

He had a tiny head, a small, delicate nose, a prim mouth, and black, thinning hair close-cropped and combed greasily straight back. That he had a heavy drinker's bearing was confirmed when he offered me a brandy and Buzz a beer. I declined for both of us, but he got up, opened a cabinet that became an elaborate bar, and poured himself a drink. He downed one in a single toss and brought a second to his chaise lounge to cuddle.

I expected the house to be filled with mementos from his long and illustrious Hollywood career, but he could have been a retired boilermaker for all the ostentation. I wondered if it was an inverted sort of vanity.

"Todd. Of course. He's missing, you say?"

"Ran away from home."

"Sorry to hear that. When did all this excitement commence?"

"A week ago."

"He was here last evening after supper," said James. "I had a little gathering, as I do some evenings. Mostly writers and artists. Young people interested in getting into film. The meager talents in this godforsaken town."

If I'd been twenty and foolish, I would have cooked up a thousand gee-whiz questions to inflate his ego, but I wasn't twenty. "Did he say anything?"

"Not that I recall." Clayton James set his brandy down on a table that was covered with lead soldiers and picked one of them up absentmindedly. "I have all the battles, you know. Waterloo. Dunkirk. Hastings."

"You collect?"

"Make and collect them. Melt the lead, detail them. It's all very time-consuming. It keeps me busy."

"I see. Nice grounds. That must take some time."

"Oh," said James flustered. "Our gardener. Carstens. Does marvelous work. You'll have to look at the grape arbor on your way out. In fact, he's been helping inside the house, too, the past few years. Dear Delores has remained a semi-invalid since her accident."

"I didn't realize . . ."

"Years ago. We really should have sued, but we were misdirected by incompetent legal counsel."

"Carstens might know where Todd went," said Buzz, sliding low on the sofa as he said it, as if to make himself into a more compact target. It seemed an unnecessary gesture until I caught the tail end of the withering look Clayton sent him.

"Yes," said Clayton, clearly annoyed at the suggestion. "I believe Carstens knows some of the youngsters. Perhaps he drove Todd to the store a time or two, running errands. Unfortunately we cannot ask him. He hasn't been working the past few days."

"He works here full time?" I asked.

"Four days a week. I'm not much for handyman jobs, Mr.

Black. In fact, lately Carstens has been preparing some of the meals. He's really quite an excellent chef."

The man's manners dominated the room like a third guest, but the city had been rife with rumors about the shenanigans at his place. I'd never been here before, but years ago some cops I knew had come on a complaint. The two cops had gotten a gander at the setup, had talked it up good. James ran informal clinics. Everybody, mostly university types and advanced high schoolers, the stray ex-beatnik, holdout hippie, struggling poet, hunkered on the floor cross-legged, while the old man perched on an ottoman and explicated upon the nature of the universe in general and the importance of his life's work in particular. Guru city.

"You *do* know who I am, don't you?"

"You wrote *The Eunuch*," I said. "Also produced and directed the film."

"I see," James said tersely. Comments shy of high praise were insults. "Anything else you wish to know?"

"Surely Todd mentioned he was having trouble at home?"

"He's spoken of that many times. In fact, Carstens was commenting upon it the other day."

"How about your wife? Could we speak to her?"

The room grew quiet. Clayton's dark eyes bore into me. "My wife has been ill."

Buzz whispered, "His wife is always ill."

"What did you say?" James asked.

"The kid wants to know where your toilet is," I said. Buzz let out an audible sigh. James knew I was lying, but he hadn't heard enough to call my bluff. He pointed the way to the lavatory, then escorted Buzz, waiting outside while the boy took care of business. I thought that was an extraordinary and freakish precaution.

When they sat down again, James straightened his jacket and crossed his legs tidily, his feet small enough to be a child's. Buzz sat closer to me than before, and it made me remember that he was still a kid.

"Anything around here turned up missing?" I asked.

"Such as?"

"I was just wondering."

"Not that I'm aware of. Todd. Todd? What is the surname again?"

"Steeb."

"Of course. Steeb *père* was here earlier in the week. The man was extremely agitated. I didn't connect the events until this moment. How very intriguing. You boys resemble your father." Beside me Buzz squirmed at the suggestion. "Funny that your question about something missing should jog my memory because he made the same inquiry. Curious, indeed."

"Is there somebody you've seen with Todd who might be able to help us, Mr. James?"

"Call me Clayton. Involved with the young man? I don't believe so. To be honest with you, we haven't seen a great deal of young Todd until the past few weeks. I don't know that he's had much of an opportunity to make friends. He did bring a girl several times, but I haven't seen her lately.

"I've had a life, Mr. Black, that lends itself to teaching the way things are. You see, I was part of the establishment, then an outcast; then I *became* the establishment. I've been beyond the blue moon and come back to tell it all. I worked, as you know, in Hollywood for many years, directing musicals and later light comedies. They said I was washed up. I decided to write a novel for the money, not any novel but a novel that would set me up for life. *The Eunuch.*

"Nobody would publish it. Said it would land us all in jail. We had it printed in Paris and smuggled copies over here. It made a splash to say the least. The Supreme Court finally called it art instead of pornography. With the movie we encountered the same problems. Financing was impossible to arrange. Too controversial. In private I was told by seven or eight producers they would love to do it, but only in a watered-down version.

"It took me five years to find somebody willing to risk the capital. My dear Delores starred."

Delores Del Rabo, rechristened Delores James in later prints of the film. If I remembered correctly, she'd married James in Mexico during the filming. There had been some scandal involved with that, too. She had been paramour to an elderly millionaire in Oregon who had been murdered by burglars under unsettling circumstances. This was back in the late fifties. The Oregon police had tried and failed to implicate her in the murder.

"It was the part of the young virgin, as you may recall. Some critics said Delores was too old. People can be very unkind."

"Yes, they can."

"Even after we finished the film, it was another six years before we started seeing returns. Nobody would play it in this country. Even now they've tried to rate it X. No justification beyond rampant jealousy. Oh, certainly a few scenes are a little suggestive, but the nudity is tasteful. No profanity. It's all alleged. It's all done by implication. That was the wonder and marvel of it, don't you see?"

"About Todd . . ."

"The trick," said Clayton, "is to write something that touches the collective unconscious of a generation. The fact that I was supposed to be washed up only made it more difficult for the Hollywood establishment to recognize what I'd accomplished. My film has been playing continuously for the last eighteen years in Europe: Paris, London, Geneva, Stockholm."

"Did Todd give you even the hint of where he might be or what he might be doing?" I asked.

James stroked his thin mustache and shook his head. "His father seems to blame me for the way his son is turning out."

A tiny bell rang in the other room, and acting like a man-servant fearful for his job, Clayton James pushed himself to his feet and scurried off to see what his wife wanted.

Buzz said, "I think he's lying."

"About which?"

"Where Todd is."

"Why would he?"

"You have to talk to his wife. You have to."

When James came back, I made the suggestion.

He said, "Delores was involved in a traffic accident twenty-five or so years ago, an accident that nearly took her life. She's been in delicate health since. Some days are better than others. I don't think so. Not today.''

A woman's tremulous voice floated from the other room. He went to her, and they spoke at some length. When he came back, he said she would see us and without a word escorted us to the door of her room, leaving us to our own introductions. But then, she had been a fixture on the silver screen for fifty years. Maybe he felt we already knew her.

The room was dark. The walls were cluttered with glass-covered photographs tracing her career from black-and-white B movies, a few character parts as a young woman with Crawford and Davis and Lombard, war films in the forties, then the decline into exploitation films and television in the fifties.

The only light in the room flickered from a huge console television in the corner, where a tag team of female wrestlers was going through their routines. Clad in lingerie meant for a vamp, she was propped up on pillows. The first thing I wondered was how many face-lifts she'd had.

10

As we entered her aerie, Buzz whispered, "Tell her you're a fan."

The air in the room was humid and hot, smelling of bad breath and chocolates and stale perfume. The old dame was tilted against half a dozen satin pillows in a huge heart-shaped bed in a room that had been enlarged after the house was built. She wore a low-cut nightgown and a smile on her rosebud lips that was as sweet as grenadine straight from the bottle. A child might mistakenly think she was in her mid-thirties; but I was in my mid-thirties, and the skin on her face was pulled tighter than mine had ever been. In the despoiling light of the TV it gave her the look of a greased mummy.

An eight-foot boa slept in coils at the foot of the bed. Her see-through nightgown was black with yellow-green feathers rimming the shoulder straps. Her hair was in disarray and dyed jet black. She'd overdosed on too many episodes of *Lifestyles of the Rich and Famous*.

In *The Eunuch* she'd played the part of a woman of twenty. Twenty-seven years ago. Except that she'd looked older at thirty-six when *The Eunuch* had been filmed than she did now. They'd done some realigning of the story to accommodate her, but it hadn't been convincing, not to any of us who had read the novel. Still, even that contrivance had not unraveled the magic of the movie for me.

A tray straddled her lap. She had been breakfasting on an enormous pile of pancakes garnished with fried eggs, sausages and sprigs of parsley. She aimed a remote-control gizmo at the TV, and killed the sound.

"Delores James," she said, holding a blue-veined hand aloft as if I might want to kiss it. I saw a sharpness in her waxy brown eyes that belied her languor. Her grip was firmer than I had a right to expect, yet the arm was like an old bone. The stand beside her bed was littered with pill bottles, mostly sleeping pills and Valium. Buzz shrank back toward the doorway.

"This is a pleasure I never thought I'd have," I lied. "I've been a fan forever. You are one of the all-time greats."

After giving me a long, cold stare, during which I grinned and held her look, she spoke in a quick, nervous patter I remembered from watching her on talk shows and *Hollywood Squares* years ago. "I have been compared with every famous actress of my generation, generally to the discredit of those actresses. It was the tragedy of Hollywood that until the end I never got the vehicles I needed to showcase my talent properly."

"I've always thought so."

"Yes."

The television distracted her long enough for me to segue into real life. "We're looking for a young man you may have met."

"I've worked with them all. Gable. Taylor. Cagney. He wrote me a fan letter not too many years ago. I have it here somewhere." She went through the motions of groping at a table opposite the one with the pill bottles, a table racked high with fanned open books, dog-eared magazines, notes, a telephone, a water glass smeared with three shades of lipstick, and an old pair of panties I didn't want to see. "He was a gentleman. They don't make men like that anymore."

"About this young man?"

She looked up. "Who, dear?"

"Todd Steeb."

"He can play that piano. He certainly can. And his girl friend. A little bitty thing. Cute as a bug's ear. I offered her a job as my maid but couldn't convince her to take it. Could have shown her how to do her makeup, a thousand things a girl needs.'' Her dark eyes grew sharp. ''I could have taught her all she needed to know about men.''

Now I knew why Buzz was uncomfortable in this place. They—Dolores and Clayton James—stared. Their eyes demanded a lot. I'd once known a moonstruck cop who stared like that, convinced that if somebody broke eye contact first, he was a burglar, masturbator, or some other villain.

''Todd, yes. He should be around tonight.''

''I don't think so. He's run away from home. We have reason to believe he's in trouble.''

''Dear. That is bad news. If he doesn't show here, I have no idea where you might find him. I'll tell you what. I'll give you a ring when he comes.'' I handed her a card even though I knew she was going to lose it. ''I don't know where he lives. Nor his little girl friend, though I asked her a number of times. Sonja is such a cutey. I'm surprised somebody hasn't pushed him down and stolen her.''

''He's been gone a week.''

''She hasn't been here with him for a while, but the way kids act these days, I'm sure they've shacked up somewhere.''

I heard a movement behind me, but Buzz had already escaped the room by the time I turned around. I heard the front door open and close.

''Todd had some trouble a couple of weeks ago. He came in here all beat up. Like the devil himself had been after him. I swear, I don't know when I've seen a kid knocked around so bad. Could barely see out of his eyes. I told him I could spruce him up with some makeup, but he wouldn't hear of it. He wouldn't tell me who'd done it. Later, when I asked Carstens, he didn't know either. Carstens used to box. He was going to show the kid a few tricks. It was the day the boy washed and waxed my Cadillac.''

''Where does Carstens live?''

I got another one of those looks. The old woman leaned over her table and popped a pill, washed it down with a gulp of juice. Valium. Then she leaned over to the table on my side and gave me a peep show I didn't need. While she futzed around in her papers, I went to the wall and began going through the old-time publicity photos. All black-and-whites except for a few taken from her television days and several from *The Eunuch*.

The newspaper clippings and fan magazine blurbs on the walls were spicy. She'd been connected at one time or another with virtually every unattached male in Hollywood and illicitly with a host of married personalities. Her private life had been legend, her career mediocre.

The south wall was nudes. Delores at eighteen. Delores at thirty-five. At forty-nine. At sixty.

It was interesting to see the inevitable deterioration in her physical plant, while the sauce and exhibitionistic streak remained unabated. Her age in the photos ranged from early twenties all the way through what could only have been last week. In its own way they were a grotesque testament to plastic surgery, silicone, body makeup, and vanity.

"Carstens," she said, still leaning toward the table, fiddling with a sheaf of curled papers. "Here it is. He lives out in Fall City, wherever that is. I never did learn Seattle like I should. Still a California girl at heart, I guess." She read me the address, and I wrote it down on my notepad. "He's got a dozen horses out there. Show horses. View of the river. Don't ask me how he can afford that sort of silly business on what we pay him. He can tell you where Todd is. They are close. Todd likes to help him in the yard. They jabber like magpies."

11

As I FIRED UP THE TRUCK AND coasted down the hill to Barton, I caught a glimpse of Clayton James standing in his open garage in full leathers, fiddling with a BMW motorcycle that looked as old as he was. He wore a prissy leather cap and goggles. He might have been taking a trip into a 1932 landscape. On the sound the wind was beginning to tease the blue waters into whitecaps. A pair of cyclists in black and yellow Lycra whizzed down the hill in front of us, spokes glittering in the sunshine.

I turned to Buzz. "You don't like her?"

"She gets bitchy. They both do. I don't know how Todd can stand them."

"Why'd you run out?"

"You were asking all the questions. You didn't need me."

"Tell me about Sonja."

"Nothing to tell."

"You called out a name when I came to your place yesterday. You thought somebody else was coming. Sonja. Your brother's girl friend."

"She used to be. I guess she still is. I dunno."

"What's she got to do with this?"

"Nothing."

I tanked up the truck at a Shell station at the corner of

Barton and Thirty-fifth, then headed for the freeway and I-90. Fall City wasn't far. I'd have a chat with Carstens.

We had already crossed Lake Washington, passing the excavation work on Mercer Island, before either of us spoke again. "Who beat Todd up?"

Buzz shrugged.

"Your father?"

"Dad wouldn't do that. Dad. I guess he's okay. When I was about ten, I used to daydream that my real father would come and get us and he'd be like this prince of a foreign country or some famous athlete playing in the majors or something like that. And he'd say, 'Hey, you guys need a bigger allowance. How about a thousand a week?' Dumb, huh?"

"None of it's dumb, Buzz. We all go through that. What happened to Todd?"

Buzz sniffed. "So we saw our real mom about two years ago. She lives in Portland, and you could tell she wanted to see us; but it didn't mean that much to her. She has eight kids, counting us. She didn't need us. She said our real father ran off after I was born—with some woman in the Army—and she hasn't seen him since. She thinks he ended up in Reno, training to be a professional gambler. Said he got shot. Was dead." He paused. "Todd got beat up, that's all. It was really . . ." Perilously close to tears, he sniffled again and got quiet.

After about a mile I said, "Who did it?"

"Sonja's dad and this other guy."

"What other guy?"

"A guy named Scotty Fogle."

"Why?"

"We were at this McDonald's on Rainier near that shopping complex on McClellan. Me and Sonja and Todd and a couple of guys from the cross-country team and another girl. I don't know her name. Mr. McCline and this Scotty Fogle came in, and you could tell they were liquored up. They spotted Sonja, and she ran over by the door to talk to her dad before he embarrassed her. But he went over to the table and

grabbed Todd by the shirt and dragged him outside in the
back. The manager called the police, but they took too long.''

"Go on.''

"Scotty Fogle held Todd's arms behind while Mr. Mc-
Cline pounded him. None of us could believe it. And Todd's
saying things like 'Why are you doing this? What did I do?'
Blood all over the place. And we're all screaming for them
to stop, but they wouldn't stop. Just kept hitting Todd.

"McCline's a big guy. Sonja said he used to be a fighter
in the Navy. You couldn't even recognize Todd after a minute. The girls were hysterical. They were all done by the
time the cops got there. The cops arrested 'em, Scotty Fogle
and McCline, but nothing ever happened. Man, you couldn't
believe it. All of us watching and nobody knowing what to
do. Sonja about went nuts, crying and shit.'' He glanced
quickly at me to see if I'd reprimand him for the last word.

"You ever find out why they did it?''

"I asked Todd, but he got weird on me. He had to get
stitches in his lip, and his face was swollen. Cracked a bunch
of ribs. He can't sleep at night they hurt so bad. He can run,
but he can't breathe very good. He's still got a little mouse.
He wouldn't talk about it. Sonja and I were going to talk
yesterday, but you came. I thought Mr. McCline might have
something to do with why he was gone.'' The boy glanced
at me, obviously hiding more than he was telling. "I just
wished I could have done something. After all the times Todd
saved me. But we just stood there, hoping it would end and
none of us knowing what to do. Anyway, they haven't seen
each other since. Sonja and Todd. McCline is strict like you
wouldn't believe.''

"He has a funny way of asking a kid not to see his daughter.''

"He's tough.''

"A tough guy would have done it with words.''

"No, he's tough.''

"The way you say that is almost as if you admire tough.''

"Don't you?''

"I've wised up in my old age. Tough is for people who
still read *Superman* comics and think Miss America would

make a really neat girl friend because she's thirty-eight—twenty-two—thirty-six. Tough isn't what I want for Christmas. It's what little, scared people want.''

Buzz didn't know how to react. He said, "McCline's brother works in the police department. We think that's why nothing ever happened. This detective with a big red nose came out and talked to us, but he pretended Todd had done something to provoke them. He kept asking us if Todd had an attitude problem. We could tell the city wasn't going to do anything. Mom and Dad . . . they didn't do anything either. They griped about it, and then they pretended to forget. Your kid gets beat to smithereens? I did something, and I'm just a kid.'' This last was said in a tiny voice.

"What'd you do, Buzz?"

"The other night I sneaked past McCline's and put eight sixteen-penny nails under his tires. Any way he went, he was going to get two flats. I'm gonna do more.''

"Is Todd planning revenge, too?"

"I dunno. Todd won't talk about it. Mr. Black—''

"Thomas.''

"He won't talk about it. We talk about everything.''

"Yeah,'' I said. "Some brothers are like that.''

Carstens had a spread east of Fall City a few miles down from Snoqualmie Falls in the valley. When we cruised through Fall City on the river, we could smell millions of ripe strawberries in the heat, could see the pickers in their straw hats hunched out in the fields. The Carstens property was all blue skies and acres of rolling pastureland, sectioned here and there by wind-bellied fencing swallowed by blackberry vines.

On the south side of the road the river flowed easily, a couple of fly fishermen in hip waders impaling the surface. On the other side a long gravel driveway led to Carstens's house.

It was a storybook house, cedar shakes on the walls and roof. The huge yard was as well groomed as the golf course we'd passed down the road. In the second pasture grazed eight or ten purebred horses, lean and shiny as chestnuts.

From the front porch you could just catch a snatch of the river beyond the road.

A white 1985 Ford pickup stood in the driveway. We knocked, but nobody answered. We tried the back. There were hills in all directions, and the air smelled of new-mown hay, horse manure, and wildflowers. It was idyllic, far nicer, I thought, than the humdrum brick palace Carstens ministered to in town.

Nobody was in back. A woodpile had been worked on, but not recently. A dog chained to a line running the length of the backyard lay under a tall birch. He didn't bark, didn't lift his chin up off his front paws. When I got close, he growled and stood, teetering this way and that.

He looked hungry.

Trouble in River City. I got a bowl of water from the back faucet and brought it over, left it a few feet from him. He waited for me to back off and lapped eagerly. I watched him stop drinking and stand guard over the bowl.

Buzz was knocking on the back door. I clomped up beside him and tried the knob. Unlocked. I thought it would be. I yelled, went inside, found the dog food under the kitchen sink, and went outside and spilled a mountain of it for the animal, along with a second bowl of fresh water. He shivered in gratitude, growled out of obligation, charged the grub, and wolfed it.

"What could have happened?" said Buzz.

"A lot of things. The old man might be upstairs with a stroke, just waiting for us to find him. Maybe he took a seven forty-seven to Katmandu, and the neighbor kid who was supposed to feed the dog forgot. Maybe this is how he treats his pets."

"I don't think so," said Buzz.

"Me neither. It doesn't fit the rest of the layout. He's done a lot of work here."

I told him to wait outside, and I went in.

Standing in the doorway, framed by the bright light outside, the boy said, "I want to come. I can see. I'm not a kid."

"You ever been fired at with a shotgun?"

"No."

"Stay there and we'll keep it that way."

It was as quaint inside as it was out. Part of a meal was curdled in a dish on the countertop. Peaches and cottage cheese. A milk container stood next to the bowl. I opened it and sniffed, almost gagged.

He wasn't in the house. I checked the bedrooms upstairs, even inspected the cellar. Nobody. I looked for a phone and found it in the kitchen, but I didn't know whom to phone. The place was decorated as if a woman had lived here once. In the living room I found a picture of her, standing alongside a tall white-haired man I took to be Carstens.

When I got outside, Buzz was standing in the front yard with his hands in his pockets, his shoulders rigid. "What's the matter?" I asked.

"I was looking around."

"Yeah."

"I went in the barn."

"Yeah."

"He wasn't there."

"You didn't find anything?"

"That's not what I'm saying."

"Keep on."

"Do dead guys stink?"

12

STEPPING GINGERLY, BUZZ LED ME across the grass to the side of the house. A well had been capped with a wooden housing, replete with a cedar shake roof, a crank, rope, and bucket. Painted brightly in blue and red, it was the sort of well you imagined fairies might flit out of. Buzz grimaced and stood back.

Although it probably filled up in the winter when the water table climbed, now it was a dry hole. Accustomed to the bright sunshine, it took a minute for my eyes to adjust, but I already knew by the odor what it was.

Deep in the cylindrical hole I spotted a pair of badly crumpled legs in coveralls, brown scuffed work boots askew.

"Carstens," I said.

"I've never seen a dead guy before."

"You have now."

"Yeah."

I looked at the boy and said, "It's hard to forget your first."

"Remember yours?" He peered down the well.

"I was a kid. She was a neighbor. I used to go over to work in her garden for small change. She was sitting in a chair, watching me. I began to wonder, after a while, why she didn't blink. When I went in and touched her, she felt like chilled clay."

78

"How old were you?"

"Eleven."

"You scared?"

"Actually I was quite scared. You're welcome to wait in the truck."

He gnawed his lip until I thought it would bleed. "I found him. I guess I'll see it through."

I thought he was making a mistake. After all, Delores James had spooked him clean out of her house with nothing more than a look. I didn't say anything. He was entitled to his own mistakes.

On the rim of the well housing I found a tack hammer and a baby food jar full of shingle nails, testimonials to a man's last chore. The lid of the jar was missing, had probably dropped in with him. There wasn't a sliver of chipped paint or a lose shingle on the premises, not a weed unpulled or branch unpruned. He'd spent his life ministering to this cheery homestead, and now it had turned on him and sucked him into a hole.

"Must have fallen," said Buzz. "When he was working on it. Landed headfirst. I guess. You think it was quick?"

"As quick as it comes."

"If it wasn't, though, can you imagine breaking your neck and laying down there, jammed upside down, waiting for help?" I could, but I didn't say so. I'd had enough close calls in my life that I didn't need to frighten myself thinking about somebody else's.

In the house I riffled the pages of his thin North Bend phone book and discovered Fall City doesn't have its own police department. King County said it'd respond to fill out the death report.

Before the police arrived, I initiated a systematic search of the house. Buzz followed me. "What are you doing?" he asked.

"I have a curious nature."

"Looking for money?"

I gave him a hard stare.

"Sorry. Don't know why I thought of that." I did. We both knew Todd was running around with bricks of hundred-dollar bills, yet neither one of us was talking about it. When the time came, I was going to have to grab this kid by the collar and shake him until his eyeballs rolled. Now wasn't the time, not when he was tripping over himself thinking about the man in the well.

Most of the furniture was fifty years old. In the corner stood a tall wooden radio that should have been in a museum. The old man had lived without frills, no reading matter except some old copies of a local newspaper featuring recipes and visits from relatives as far away as Mount Vernon and Tacoma. A well-thumbed family Bible. Seed catalogs marked and inked up for reference. His closets were as bare as a traveling salesman's. No TV. A 1950 plastic tube radio in the kitchen. The phone was on a short leash in a nook with no chair nearby.

I wondered what he did for kicks. Weed the nasturtiums? Spit cherry pits off the back porch? On the way out of the kitchen I spotted something in a corner beyond the door.

A battered envelope, empty, addressed to Carstens. The return address was missing, only a name in its place, scripted with a fountain pen. Leona Galloway. The name was unfamiliar to me. Buzz read it over my shoulder without comment.

I couldn't quite make out the postmark, but the stamp wasn't one I'd seen in a spell. I folded the envelope in quarters and pushed it into my shirt pocket.

"You going to keep it?" Buzz asked.

"Probably just garbage."

Trailing a cloud of dust, two white King County police cars showed up and deposited a litter of polite men in brown uniforms.

After they had peered into the well with flashlights, we gathered around and discussed how we were going to fish him out. Eventually we called the Fall City Fire Department, and the fire fighters eased a ladder from the ramshackle barn-garage into the well, then looped a noose around his ankles. It was macabre—cranking the well handle and watching a dead man come up feet first.

Wearing latex gloves and particle masks, fire fighters laid

Carstens out on the grass, and then we all stood around looking sage and tried to guess how long. Three, four days was the consensus. Clayton James said he hadn't been to work for a few days. Small wonder.

Except for gashes on the head and an oddly bent neck, there were no wounds. Rigor mortis had come and gone. The well had kept him cool enough so that the heat hadn't fully had her way with him. He was the man in the photo in the living room. Carstens.

In their brown wool shirts the two county police commiserated with Buzz and me, assumed we were relatives. I didn't bother to set them straight. I noticed three of the cops stood in the shade of a small maple while the other sweated in the sun. He said, "Damn shame we can't all die on our hundredth birthday."

Another cop said, "I'd like to try for about a hundred and two myself."

A third liked the sport. "Me? I want to go at sixty-five. In the saddle on somebody else's filly." He shot a guilty look around the group, having forgotten the boy.

A dusty, wrinkled man who should have been duded up in cowboy rigging and pasted onto a cigarette billboard sauntered toward us from the east across a field and told us he'd warned Carstens. Phil Stains was a neighbor. He seemed kindly enough, too weary to be mean.

He kept shaking his head, avoiding the uniformed men with his dull brown eyes as if he'd been in trouble with the law before. "Should have sold me this place when I offered ten years ago. That Carstens. Always secretive. Lived next to him over thirty years and never knew what he ate for breakfast. Had them racehorses he was fatting up for his nephew. Never did wanta tell nobody. I guess it embarrassed him knowing how much they was worth. His nephew dragged 'em out here 'cause he was gettin' a divorce. Hidin' property from the little woman."

We all looked across the pasture at the grazing horses. Phil Stains wore cowboy boots broken down at the heels, khaki trousers, and a flannel shirt that looked as if it'd been dragged behind a mule. It was a balmy day, but he wore long johns underneath and rivaled Carstens for gamy.

"One of the oldest houses in the valley," Stains said. "'Bout 1880. Carstens's great-grandfather put it up. Been in the family ever since. Came out here to mine gold but gave it up. Lot of folks came out here to dig gold. Never was enough to fill a bad tooth."

I said, "Carstens have any visitors this week?"

"Seem to me there was," said Stains. "Seem to me there was." We all watched while he tried to rope a thought. "Yeah, some young feller. I 'member now, 'cause he asked the wife if we was the Carstens place."

"Wasn't driving a '53 Studebaker, was he?"

"How the heck did you know that? She was a beauty. I believe that buggy had the original whitewalls on her. Sounded like a cylinder was starting to miss, though."

"Do you know what the guy in the Studebaker wanted with Carstens?"

"Heck, we mind our own business out here. I never paid it no mind till you asked." Phil Stains stared out at the horses again, and what little light there had been behind his brown eyes extinguished itself.

After we'd explained to King County why we'd been out there and we all speculated aloud how it was a sad sort of accident to happen to an old man, Buzz and I climbed back into my Ford and headed back to town. We detoured through Issaquah and had lunch at the local Skipper's.

Buzz ate heartily. "Run a ways this morning?" I asked.

"Twelve. Not bad."

"You want more chow, it's on me."

"Nah."

"Out prowling last night, weren't you?"

"Me?"

"You look sleepy."

"I had a friend drive me back to Chinatown after dinner. I thought Todd would come back. You know, his sleeping bag and all."

"Did he?"

"We went up there with flashlights about eleven o'clock,

and everything was the same. Waited around, but we couldn't very well stay all night. Besides, it was kind of spooky. I don't know how he can stay there.''

''You know where else he might be?''

''Might have slept in his car. He's done that before when he had fights with Dad.'' Buzz watched me finish a platter of fish and chips. ''You seen a lot of dead guys, Mr. Black?''

''A few.''

''Kind of creepy, huh?''

''A lot just look like they're asleep. In fact, most do. Ever meet Carstens when he was alive?''

He nodded.

''What was he like?''

''He never said anything to me. Todd said he talked to him, but I don't see how. Never said a word that I saw. He was quieter than me, you know, like it hurt for him to talk.''

''Does it hurt you to talk?''

''Sometimes. I read once in *Reader's Digest* about people dying and then coming back, you know, like a doctor gave them shocks or something. They were like floating in the room, watching their own bodies and the nurses. They were still there. Or their spirit was. Or something. When we were out there looking at Carstens, I kept thinking his spirit was floating around and he could hear what we were saying, and I wanted to say something nice about him but I couldn't think of a thing.''

''I've had that feeling,'' I said. ''Come on. I'm going to buy you something.''

''Me?''

We drove through Issaquah until we found a Pay 'n Save across from the freeway. In the parking lot Buzz craned his neck around, watching a trio of high parachutists dropping toward the sky park across I-90. In just a few weeks the park would be closed so somebody could slap up another business park. I bought the boy an electric razor. At first he pinked up and demurred. ''Not for me,'' he said.

''Your parents are paying for it. Go on. If you're old enough to use it, you're old enough to need it.''

''Me?''

"Unless you're trying to grow a mustache."

"No, sir."

"No, Thomas. Directions are inside."

"Thanks . . . Thomas."

On the way back to Seattle I thought he was going to loosen up and tell me the rest of what he knew about his brother, but he didn't. I spoke over the snore of the wind on my truck windows. "Don't you think it's about time we met up with Sonja?"

"Huh?" I noticed him staring at the pocket that held the envelope from Carstens's kitchen.

"Todd's girl friend. Don't you think it's about time I met her?"

He nodded, looking as if he were about to take a first-ever roller coaster ride, and not too sure about it.

"She go to Franklin with you guys?"

"Yeah."

"What time does school let out?"

"Two-fifteen."

"We'll just make it."

He nodded again.

"This is okay with you, Buzz?"

"Yeah. Sure. Why wouldn't it be?"

13

FRANKLIN HIGH SCHOOL HAD ITS seventy-fifth reunion and anniversary last year. Constructed of brick and mortar and hardwood floors with thirty years of wax on them, the building was massive, overshadowing the neighborhood like a buxom old maid.

I hadn't gone there, but plenty of friends and acquaintances had. These days the student body was an amalgam of Asians, blacks, Samoans, and whites. Busing was still going strong in Seattle, and the orange steel and glass transports lined up under the shade trees on the slope of Mount Baker Boulevard, nose to butt, awaiting the rowdy troops. We were early. Following directions, I double-parked across from the north entrance to the school. Buzz knew Sonja's habits as well as any admiring swain would.

Toting textbooks and a knapsack, she strolled along in the hubbub alongside two girl friends, both black and pretty. When they got close, Buzz jumped out and spoke in a hoarse whisper. "Sonja? Sonja?"

"Hey, Buzz," she said.

"Sonja? Can you talk to us?"

She looked me over. Half Asian and half white, wide of face, with almond-shaped eyes so dark they were almost black, she had dyed her hair a strange shade of orange-brown, cut it in what used to be called a China Chop, and then haphazardly moussed it to her own taste. Despite the indiscretion, she was attractive.

She said, "This the detective you were telling me about?" Still clutching the package we'd purchased in Issaquah, Buzz nodded. One of the black girls giggled at Buzz in a teasing way, but he didn't notice, and she didn't do it again. When she had finished appraising me, Sonja said, "Sure. What do you want?"

"A half hour."

"I guess."

"I'm trying to find Todd. I have reason to believe he's in trouble."

She looked at Buzz, and a signal of some sort passed between them. Bidding good-bye to her friends, she climbed in beside the boy. "Thomas Black," I said.

"Sonja McCline." She dropped cautious and picked up bubbly. "I know. Funny name. Sonja and McCline don't exactly go together. And I'm half Japanese on top of that. My mother married a GI and needed to Americanize everything in the worst way. Mom thought Sonja was an American name because a nurse in the hospital where I was born was named Sonja. So here I am. Ta-daaaah."

Buzz locked his door beyond Sonja and fastened his seat belt tidily. He said, "We found a dead guy this afternoon."

The girl's cheeks sagged as she turned first to him, to me, then back to him. "Who?"

"Mr. Carstens. Remember? From Clayton James's house? The old guy who kept serving everybody drinks and stuff. His hands kept shaking? The old lady used to snap at him."

"He died?"

"Fell down a well."

"Gosh."

"I discovered him."

"Todd wasn't hanging around, was he?"

"Not so anybody could tell," I said.

"It was all to do with his uncle," she said.

"Who?"

"Todd's Uncle Jan."

We ended up at the same McDonald's where Todd Steeb

had been bruised up by Sonja's father. I sprang for soft drinks and a pair of hamburgers for Buzz's bottomless pit, and we settled down at a table near the front windows. During our drive and while ordering at the front, Sonja had been looking me over rather artfully.

She had plump cheeks and a figure that verged on chubby. Short. She wore long tan shorts and a very tight black sleeveless shirt. She didn't have a clue how pretty she was. She was a talker. A worrier. You could see years of tension molding her squared-off shoulders.

"You been going with Todd long?" I asked.

"A year. But I'm not going with him." She sipped on her cola. "I mean I am, but I'm not. Officially I'm not. My father won't let me see him. But I'm a senior. I'm getting a job this summer. Pretty soon I'll have an apartment and a car of my own."

"Meaning?"

"Dad won't be bossing me around anymore."

"He'll try," said Buzz.

"Sure. But he can't be everywhere."

"What do you know about Todd running away?" I asked.

"Everybody in school heard. It's like he's the big mystery kid. Nobody knew anything about him until he played the piano at that talent contest last year. Just wasted everybody. He played classical, old stuff he called boogie-woogie, rock'n roll, jazz. Like he was a genius or something. Everybody wanted to be friends with him and were inviting him to parties and all that stuff, and he didn't care a bit. He never went to one party.

"I even had a teacher mention him. She said he was neglecting his God-given talents, like not getting an A in biology. That he was going nowhere. At seventeen Todd's already better on a piano than she'll ever be as a teacher. His dad's trying to make him work in the plant driving a forklift for eight dollars an hour. He's wonderful, Mr. Black."

"Call him Thomas," said Buzz, grinning at me through a mouthful of hamburger. I smiled at his puppy-dog look.

"Why does your father dislike Todd so much?"

Noisily she sipped from her straw. She sighed heavily, and

everything slumped except the blocky shoulders. She peered out the spotless window at some kids on the street. "The deal is, my dad's never liked anybody I've gone with. My first boyfriend was like Japanese, and my dad said I couldn't go out with any Japs. And I'm half Japanese! David was scared of him and too polite to defy him or anything, so I just never saw David again. My dad's very possessive. Ever known anybody like that?"

"A few. Why'd he beat on Todd?"

"You're not going to believe this."

"Give me a try."

She took a deep breath. "He thought Todd was rattling me." I must have given her a questioning look because she explained immediately. "Sex. You know. He thought we were having sex." Buzz blushed and turned away, trying hard not to be part of the conversation. "But we weren't. Not like he thought. But you don't tell my dad anything. He decided we were sleeping together, and he spoke to Todd about it. I was so embarrassed. Then that weekend he found us here. I thought he was going to cripple Todd. He's crippled people. He breaks their knees so they can never walk again. I hated him."

"You don't anymore?"

"He's just—He can't honestly help what he is, Mr. Black. My father . . . he'll never change. I feel sorry for him, at least I do when he's not making me miserable. You see, my mother died when I was about a year old, and he's never been much for kids. Grandma came and lived with us and more or less raised me until about a year ago. By then his drinking got so bad and the squabbling so loud Grandma gave up and moved to Tacoma with her sister. I wanted to go, too, but I would have had to leave Todd, switch high schools in my senior year, and all.

"I haven't seen him for weeks. Not since Dad and Scotty beat him up."

"Nice ring," I said, casually. She looked down at her hand, self-consciously modeling it so the light could glint off it. It was an antique, gold, inset with green-tinted jewels that I figured could be either emeralds or cut glass.

"Dad took it away and went and had it analyzed or whatever."

"Appraised," said Buzz, avoiding my eyes. His throat was dry. "You don't have to tell him this stuff."

"Appraised. Todd gave it to me. It turned out it was worth like five thousand dollars or something. So my dad was going to take it to Todd's dad and ask him where he got it. I swiped it before he could. Been hiding it ever since. I have a place cut out inside a book where I keep it."

"The Eunuch?"

"Nancy Drew. Dad took my copy of *The Eunuch* and burned it."

"Couldn't your father guess who took the ring?"

"I took it out of his glove box when he was in the J and M, used his other car keys. He thought somebody stole it. You know, the whole thing is funny. Really. If you think about it. My dad never listens to anything I say anyway. I gave up a long time ago. I'm just waiting to get enough saved up to leave. I'm eighteen. I can go anytime. I almost sold this ring so I could get a car, but Todd told me I had to keep it."

"Where'd Todd get it?"

"From his grandmother, or something. I'm not sure." As she spoke, Buzz Steeb bumped her thigh under the table and made a face. Whatever he was hinting at, she didn't get it. "I know what Todd's doing, Mr. Black. I know why he took off."

It made me feel incredibly ancient to hear high school kids calling me mister. "Why did Todd take off?"

"He's investigating his uncle's suicide. Supposed suicide. Six years ago. You see, his father doesn't want him to. They had a couple of knock-down-drag-outs over it. Course, it was more than just the uncle thing. I mean, Todd's been having more and more trouble with his dad the last year. I mean his dad never did appreciate what he could do on a piano. And then, when he got beat up, his dad seemed to blame him. Didn't he, Buzz?"

"I guess."

"When Todd quit the track team, it seemed to his father as if he was cracking up."

"Was he?"

Buzz shook his head. "But he blamed Todd for my quitting. Like it was Todd's decision. Only Todd told me to stay."

"You see," continued Sonja, "Todd found out his uncle was doing some sort of research, writing a book."

"On Clayton James?"

"Did Buzz tell you?"

I looked over at the boy. "That was a wild guess. Buzz left a few things out."

"So Todd's been spying on James. And his dad found out. It really ticked him off. And Clayton James? It was weird. We just walked into his house one evening. The place was full of these strange people who sat around and took notes on everything James said. And his wife? Yuck. She knew me about ten minutes when she wanted me to move in and be her maid. Can you believe it? I was supposed to sleep on the rug in her room in case she needed something in the middle of the night like a slave or something." She rolled her eyes. "It was just too—too weird."

"What did Todd find?"

"His uncle's notes. Tons of them. I didn't read them all. About the movie Clayton James made of *The Eunuch*. He had all kinds of tidbits. Really dumb stuff like the name and address of the bookkeeper on the movie project. The name of the son of the guy who did all the stunts. Stuff like that."

I looked at Buzz. "Where'd Todd get your uncle's papers?"

"After Grandma had her stroke, most of her stuff was sent to charities, but she had this one trunk stored at our house in the closet under the basement stairs. We didn't even know it was there until Grandma let it out one day a couple of months ago—Easter Sunday. He went into it and broke the lock and like found all this stuff. I don't know what he did with it when he ran away."

"I don't know all of what Todd found, Mr. Black," said the girl. "But I know his uncle discovered Clayton James was more bizarre than anybody knew. If he'd finished his book, it would have unmasked him."

"Will your dad be home this afternoon?" I asked.

"Probably. He runs McCline Towing but only spends his mornings there and sometimes late at night. He's an alcoholic, Mr. Black." She searched my face to see what effect her announcement had. "Scotty's his drinking buddy, and he's an alcoholic, too. Functional alcoholics, I guess they call them. Don't hit the taverns until about six. Then it's the J and M up on Rainier when they really need it. They don't like that place 'cause it's all black except them, but they wind up there. Or they'll go downtown. Sometimes out to Ballard. He doesn't know where Todd is."

"He knows why he beat him up."

"We all know that. He's just mean."

"I'd like to ask him."

"Just, please, don't tell him you were talking to me."

"That goes without saying."

14

THE MAN WHO ANSWERED THE DOOR probably hadn't processed more than a single beer today, yet he staggered. When he wasn't shuffling from foot to foot in the doorway, his eyes staggered, too. Thin and wiry, he was about five inches taller than I was, which would have put him at six-feet-six, and maybe fifteen to twenty years older—in his early fifties. He had enough hair for two men, cut young and loose and worn carelessly. His sandy handlebar mustache hovered over a smirk.

He'd spilled something that looked like ink in the center of his white V-neck T-shirt. A walking Rorschach. His smiling eyes were the pale brown color of mountain dirt.

"Who?" he said.

"McCline."

"Ain't here." I knew he was lying, but it wasn't his tone or his face that betrayed him.

"How about his daughter?"

"Ain't here neither." The house was on Thirty-fourth Avenue South—once an exclusive neighborhood, now gone to pot. It was a couple of blocks shy of having a view of Lake Washington. The siding needed paint; the yard was unkempt. A rusted-out wheelbarrow half full of dissolved dirt clods and rainwater stood in the work position, waiting for somebody to come back from a break started last summer.

"I know McCline's here. If it's all the same to you, I'll wait."

"Okay. He's here. He's tired, and I figured he'd appreciate it if I sent you away. Who should I say is calling?"

"Thomas Black. I'm a private investigator."

"Creeper peeper, huh?" said the skinny man, his voice beginning to lose its friendly music. Beside me, Buzz was immobile.

"Just call McCline, would you, please?"

He grinned and showed enough food in his teeth to feed the cat for a week. "Maybe McCline ain't talkin' to wise guys today."

"He can't talk to anybody if we don't ask him, can he?"

Despite his height and his sass, the man appeared harmless. His innocuous look brought the whole sad, infuriating story of the beating they'd given Todd Steeb back to me. It worked on my patience like a sizzling fuse. Without knowing how it had come over me, I realized I hadn't been this angry in a long while. I hoped I didn't do anything stupid before I squeezed some information out of these two birds.

"Maybe McCline and I got better things to do than gab with a peeper. Like watch videos of trout fishing on the moon."

"I think McCline'd be ticked off if he missed this opportunity to talk to the investigator who's looking for the missing kid you two messed up a few weeks back."

That took him aback. "The kid at McDonald's? We never did what they said. Nobody beat him up."

"He went to the hospital."

"We don't know nothin'. I hardly remember his name. We made a mistake, okay. We didn't mean to hurt nobody."

"I'm sure he remembers it different."

"Maybe. But that whole thing never should have happened."

"You really forgot his name? He remembers yours. Scotty Fogle."

Scotty gave me a startled look, which he managed to convert into a smirk again before he trotted off through the house.

McCline and Fogle carried beers back into the living room. Fogle waved me in through the still-open front door.

Big and heavy, McCline was all chest. His arms were as swollen as cooked sausages. A couple inches shorter than I was, he weighed an easy 240. He was blond, blue-eyed, with a crew cut, a man who'd never given the cut up after the Marines. Or was it the Navy? Sure. On top of the television was a picture of him in swabbies, and another of him on the wall with his arm twined around a small Japanese woman. They both were younger, and McCline was trimmer; but the meanness in the little porcine eyes was evident even then.

Today he wore natty loafers, polyester pants, and a yellow shirt with a bird stitched over the left breast. He could have been a golf pro.

"Yeah," he said, inspecting me as he sat heavily in the center of a couch. Fogle draped himself crossways over an easy chair. Neither of them offered us a seat.

I couldn't help myself. "I understand you like to beat up kids."

McCline's eyes turned into BBs as he slurped from the Budweiser can. "This about that Steeb punk? Who's this shitass? The little brother? You got your facts wrong if you think we beat him up. He might have got hurt a little, but we didn't beat him up. Who said we did?"

"People who know."

"He put his little nose where it shouldn't have been. What's it to ya?"

"I'd like to know why."

'Who the fuck are you? Why? Get out of here. What makes you think I'll tell you how many hairs on a gnat's ass? You a cop? Get out of here."

"Private investigator," said Fogle, enunciating the words in a manner that, under other circumstances, would have made me laugh.

"Like the kid can't take care of his own messes? When you find him, tell him next time he runs into the big boys, he better turn tail and run his ass out of there."

"What I like about this whole business," I said, "what I

like is it took two of you. A seventeen-year-old kid. It would be laughable if it wasn't so pathetic.''

"You think I couldn't take *you* alone?"

"We're not talking me. We're talking about two grown men against a boy who weighs about as much as a line of laundry after a June rain."

"Two of us, you say?" McCline scratched his inner thigh, and it sounded like a woman scratching a nylon stocking. "I coulda handled him with one hand tied behind my back. But I ain't gonna go chasing around some parking lot."

"He's missing. Did you know that? I think it has something to do with you slamming him around."

McCline took another long draft and thought that over. "He's really missing?"

"For over a week."

McCline's tone altered, and it surprised me. "Sorry to hear that. I am. Whatever else, the kid's got guts. He ain't no brawler, but he's got guts. I'll hand him that. He took it like a man . . . not that I'm admitting anything. Nobody's filing charges, and I want to keep it that way. So what's this got to do with me?"

"I want to know if you've seen him since that night."

"Why would I?"

"Okay, you haven't seen him. Why'd you beat him up?"

"Nobody's admitted to beating nobody. Understand? I'm trying to be decent, you know, do the decent thing here, but I don't have to answer these questions."

"I realize that."

"Well, so why'd the kid get hurt?"

"Yeah."

"I warned him to keep away from my little girl. I warned him, and you know what he said to me? Said, 'It's a free country.' I couldn't believe that shit. So I tied one on and did something I'm ashamed of. Okay? I'm not saying I touched a hair of his head. But I did make a mistake. There. Happy?"

"There's more to it."

"What are you getting at?"

"You were planning to talk to his father, weren't you? Until somebody stole a ring from you."

"How do you know about that?"

"I've been asking around."

"I know nothin' about no ring."

"We can get the police back here."

"The cops know me. I don't sneak around. I do my shit in the open."

"What'd you tell Todd when you warned him away from your daughter?"

McCline was sitting upright, gulping down the last of his beer. Fogle had altered positions but didn't seem interested in uncoiling from his chair. Before speaking, McCline tightened up his neck muscles and jutted his chin out, as if his tie were too tight, except he wasn't wearing a tie.

"Look," he said. "You think you're so brilliant? You know as well as I do them damn kids are ripping this town apart. And the reason is we got so many goddamned fucking liberal pantywaists like you running around singing the blues about their rights. Me? When I was his age, if I'd defied my elders like he did, I'd've got my brains stove in. The way I see it, he got off lucky."

"His mother thinks he's going to kill himself."

For a moment I thought I saw a flicker of remorse behind his bright blue eyes, but it was betrayed by his words. "Ain't nothing to do with me. Life is hell. The sooner these little bastards learn that, the better off they'll be. They can't take it and bail out, that's their problem."

"I didn't think they made guys like you anymore," I said, sarcasm bleeding into my voice.

His hammy hands curled into fists, and he planted his legs; but he didn't get up or move on me. Because he kept scanning my clothing, I was reasonably certain the reason McCline hadn't already laid hands on me was he thought I was carrying.

"Tell you what, shitheel," whispered McCline, crinkling his blue eyes and compressing his lips. "You know where I am. You think I'm such a pushover, you come back and try it. Anytime."

"I'll check my calendar."

"I just bet you will."

When we got inside the truck, Buzz glowered at me. I said, "What?"

He came close to bursting into tears. "I thought you were tough."

"You've been watching too many movies, Buzz."

"I bet you know karate or something. I bet you would have knocked all his teeth out on the rug."

"Tough is the wrong thing to try to be, Buzz."

He pondered that. "So what do you admire in a man?"

"Try compassion for a start."

"That's stupid. That's something women have." I looked over at him, wondering whether I had been that blunt and naive as a fourteen-year-old. He was quivering, mouth agape, scrawny mustache splotching the white of his upper lip. He was incensed that I hadn't drawn blood, and to make matters worse, here I was rebuking his vision of the world.

"You have compassion, Buzz," I said gently. "It's one of the things I like about you."

A few moments later, when I still hadn't moved the truck, he said, "Man, you see all those boxing pictures on the wall in the hallway? That guy's hands are lethal weapons. Scotty Fogle looks like nothing, but he'll get in it. Sonja said her dad gets into a ton of fights and Scotty always helps. They put a guy in the hospital last year. What would you've done if he'd a taken a swipe at you?"

I smiled patiently. "Let's talk about something else."

"It was the first time I've seen them since they did Todd. I just kept thinking about it, the way they took their time, like they knew nobody could stop them. Todd didn't even put up a fight. He kept saying, 'What are you doing, Mr. McCline? Why are you doing this? Sir?' He called him sir. You could see this dazed look on McCline's face. I think it got to him."

We sat in the truck two doors up from McCline's house, and I watched a fly bang his head against the inside of the windshield. Buzz didn't stir. I was beginning to doubt Sonja's contention that her father had punched out her boyfriend from pure meanness.

McCline's former offices in Chinatown had recently been burgled by Todd Steeb. The boy was sleeping in an abandoned hotel situated directly over them. McCline had confiscated and then had appraised a ring Todd had given Sonja. Todd's uncle had once worked for McCline Towing. In addition, Todd's uncle had committed suicide in the same block where he had once worked for McCline Towing. And now, prowling Chinatown, Todd was investigating his uncle's suicide.

I said, "Todd started seeing Sonja so he could spy on her old man, didn't he?"

"Don't tell Sonja. He really got to like her."

"So who knows the most about your uncle Jan?"

"You're going to investigate his death?" Buzz asked, a note of hope brightening his words.

"Todd is, and Todd's missing. Like I said before, I'm a curious type."

"Grandma. She knew Uncle Jan."

"Over the hills and through the woods?"

"Just a couple of miles."

15

THE WARM AIR WAS LADEN WITH THE aroma of peanut butter cookies, Pine Sol, medicine, and old people. Buzz trotted into the place, giving a sweet hello to a hefty, knock-kneed black woman swinging a mop. He scrawled his signature in a guest book at the front counter, galloped down a corridor, and rapped at a door beyond the kitchen. Before I could catch him, he vanished.

The nursing home was on Martin Luther King Junior Way, in the heart of the Central District, a gargantuan four-story home built around 1910, remodeled inside but not out.

The hardwood floors had been scuffed into disrepute before most of the residents had graduated from grade school. The rooms were wallpapered, the woodwork and doors painted a sickly pale green. I passed a communal television room lined with blank-eyed inmates, all elderly. Only one looked up from a game show.

Three brass beds sectioned off the room like caskets, each painted a different gaudy enamel color: red, peacock blue, canary yellow. Three wooden bureaus and three chairs, painted to match the bed frames, completed the decor. Personal items were few: a pair of reading glasses in a tattered case; a paperback book by Erle Stanley Gardner; a vase with a single wilted peony in it. The mattresses on the beds sagged. They bore hand-sewn quilts. Two women occupied the room, one fat and smiling, her white arms bare.

The other was Buzz's grandmother.

A wizened old dame, she was thinner than her daughter, Faith, and probably forty years older. Goatlike hairs sprouted out of several moles on her face. Her upper lip needed shaving. The little knob at the end of her protruding chin was flat enough to put a thimble on. Grandmother sat in a chair, Buzz on the swaybacked bed across from her, holding her hand. The old woman had a thick glaze in her eyes as if they had been baked in a kiln.

"This is Grandma Galloway," Buzz said, quietly.

"Leona," I said. "Leona Galloway."

Astonished, Buzz asked, "How did you know that?"

I lifted the envelope I'd picked up from the kitchen floor in Fall City partially out of my shirt pocket, then jammed it back in.

"Oh, yeah."

"Oh, yeah."

"I'm sorry."

"You haven't been coming clean with me, have you, Buzz?"

"I don't have to now. You know everything I do." We kept our eyes on his grandmother, watched her take a deep breath and blow. She was not responding.

"The money," I said to Buzz.

The boy scratched his elbow. "I don't know how much Todd had. I should have told you about it, but he made me promise. He doesn't trust anybody right now. Not even me. I guess he's right, though."

"What do you mean?"

"Here I am telling you."

"Where did he find this money?"

"He wouldn't say."

"Chinatown?"

"I thought you knew that much. But I don't know where."

"Whose money is it?"

"Uncle Jan's."

"Drug money?"

"I don't think Uncle Jan would have done anything like that. But I was pretty young when he went away. I guess a kid doesn't really know what a grown-up might do. Mrs. Hendrickson," said Buzz to the fat lady across the room, "has Grandma been herself this morning?"

Rosebud lips pursed, the fat lady in the other chair smiled angelically. "Not this morning."

Buzz spanked his grandmother's hand gently and said, "Grandma? Grandma? It's me. Grandma?" She came around slowly, and we all sat and waited as if we were waiting for a shooting star on the hottest night of the year. We had nothing else to do. Nobody else to chase. There was a dead man in Fall City and a missing boy in Chinatown, and this addlepated old lady was going to solve the riddle.

The boy looked at me and said, "She had a stroke six years ago. Right after Jan died. When she had the stroke, she fell down a flight of stairs. It was two days before anybody found her. She's been here ever since."

"Elroy? Is that my Elroy?"

"Grandma, how are you today?"

"I wonder I'm okay. Is it Monday?"

"Wednesday, Grandma."

"Goodness, how the time does fly."

"I brought a man to talk to you, Grandma. About Uncle Jan."

She turned to me but couldn't quite focus her pinprick blue eyes. Hairs grew out of her eyelids. Her liver-colored lips belonged on some sort of sea mammal.

"Dear Jan was always getting into jams. I remember, it was September, 1944, and Jan came home from school with a note from his teacher. He'd been wasting his whole day making goo-goo eyes at a new girl. Thatcher, I believe her name was. Peggy, or Susie? It was Megan. Megan Thatcher. Mrs. Rosenthal really gave him heck. Genevieve Rosenthal, married to our neighbor's cousin Harold. I attended the wedding. Wore an organdy dress. A June wedding. It was such a nice day, the day Jan came home with that note. On lined notebook paper. Green lines. Green ink. It was the fifteenth of the month. A Friday. You know how Septembers can be in Seattle.''

"I know," I said. "I'm trying to find out about your son, Jan. He was planning to write something about *The Eunuch*, wasn't he?''

"My, my, Jan was always writing something. What day did you say this was, Elroy?''

"Wednesday.''

She peered around, trying to orient herself. "Have I had breakfast?''

"You must have, Grandma. It's almost time for dinner.''

"I guess I must. What year is it? Seventy-three?''

Gently Buzz told her how far off she was.

"Golly whee.''

I'd seen people like her before, people who could recall the color of the sunset and the price of Boraxo seventy years ago yet not know what they'd had for lunch.

"About your son, Jan?'' I said.

The only part of her anatomy that moved was her dry mouth.

"Jan was always the yakker. Always full of big plans. Wanted to start his own business and be somebody. Well, I guess he fetched that dream ta home. It was 1959, and he didn't have a red cent. December twentieth, a Sunday night. He came to me and asked me to go along with his tale. I don't lie, but I did for Jan. And then I didn't hear another word about the filthy business until the week before he died. That was . . . when was that? But then, that whole time is so fuzzy. They say I had a stroke. You'd think a body'd recall a stroke.''

"What was Jan's lie?''

"Oh, you'll have to ask Jan that, won't you?''

"Jan is dead," I said. She focused her kiln-dried blue on her grandson and thought about it for a few moments. "Of course, he is. Of course. Dead. Terrible thing for the whole family. Especially these two boys. Elmore was always thinking up some new theory about why the earth was spinning; Elroy always with mush on his face. They worshiped their uncle Jan. A body hates to lose a son that way.''

"What was Jan's lie, Mrs. Galloway?"

She worked her false teeth around inside her elastic lips and then planted them back where they belonged. "How did you know about that?"

"You just told me."

"Don't know why I would do that."

"Todd's missing. Your grandson has disappeared, and I think it has something to do with your son's lie."

"It was the money. He paid off my house. Eight thousand dollars. Gave it to me cash. Just put the money in my hand like a cold biscuit. I was afraid to walk out of the front door. I pulled the shades, turned off the lights, locked the doors, and sat up with it all night." She rolled her eyes and twitched her lips, moving a gnarled hand in her lap. Buzz hadn't let go of her. Even though his grandmother's personality had been whitewashed by time and accident, Buzz could see the colors of his old granny bleeding through.

"It was 1959," she said. "Yes, or was it '60? No, it wasn't an election year. I remember I voted for Nixon. Couldn't abide a Catholic in office. It was '59. December. The weather was sloppy. I had a nice home over on Angeline Street.

"I was to tell anybody who asked that I'd loaned Jan and his brother-in-law, Dudley, an undisclosed amount of money to start a business. They weren't brothers-in-law then, of course. From my savings. Know what I had in savings? Five hundred and fifty-three dollars. It cost a hundred and twelve dollars to get the furnace fixed. Scrimping on my husband's railroad pension. Faith used to give me money once a month. Always a good daughter."

"How much money were you supposed to have loaned them, Mrs. Galloway?"

"Loaned?"

"Jan and Dudley."

"I have no idea. Besides, I shouldn't have let on this much. Jan will be cross."

"Where did Jan get it? The cash."

"Came in one evening, a Sunday it was, in the rain . . . Remember he tracked mud all over my kitchen linoleum.

Flying from pillar to post. And chattering away. Something had happened. Then he handed me all that wet cash.''

"Wet?"

"Don't you see? It had been out in the rain with him."

The white-haired fat lady across the room got up and shuffled out of the room behind a clomping aluminum-framed walker, the rubber cleats squeaking on the polished floor. "I don't need to sit here and listen to her pull the wool over your eyes, mister. I guess I know a tall tale when I hear one."

After she had gone, I said, "Where is the money now. Mrs. Galloway?"

"Jan's money? I suppose it's with Jan."

"He passed away."

"I remember now. Right before he died. He wanted me to do something. It's hell to get old and feel all your plumbing fall apart. He wanted me to . . . I know." Her eyes lit up with the sudden clarification. "Jan wanted to give the money back. That was it. He was going to give back every red cent."

"Didn't Dudley have anything to say about it? I mean they would have had to take the money out of the business, wouldn't they?"

"Dudley?" Then she was gone for a few minutes, staring.

"It wears her out," said Buzz. "She can talk and everything, but it really wears her out."

"That your brother over there?" I said, gesturing to a small stand next to her bed.

Buzz picked up a framed photo and passed it to me. It was a shot of a brown-haired lad of about fourteen sitting on a concrete sea wall in shorts. From the look of his legs he had been running even then. The old lady spoke from her trance. "That was before the scars."

"Scars?"

"The dog," said Buzz, looking grim.

"Tell me about it."

"I was ten and he was fourteen and we were down by the lake one day and pair of Dobermans came up out of the grass after me and I started screaming and Todd ran over and threw me behind him. I peed my pants I was so scared. He kept going around in circles, holding me behind while those dogs went at him. He never flinched, just kept holding me.''

"A brave, brave boy," said the old woman. "Both my boys are brave." She clutched Buzz's hand so hard it turned white and he had to wrench it away. "But especially Elmore. The dogs' owner went into shock when she saw Elmore's face. At first they thought he'd never be the same, but they got a brilliant plastic surgeon. You can hardly tell. Another operation or two, and you won't be able to.''

"No, Grandma," said Buzz. "You can tell. And Todd swore off any more operations." He turned to me. "It's not that bad really. The left side of his face. Three big smooth scars from here to here. They had me by the stomach and weren't going to let go. The medics said Todd saved my life. And then Todd was in surgery all night. I cried. I was out way before him, and I thought for sure he'd died and nobody was telling me.''

"My brave, brave boys," said the old lady.

"Mind if I borrow this picture, Mrs. Galloway?"

During ten minutes of reasoning Buzz and I failed to convince her—she losing time and place all the while—until she zoned out and I took it. I tried one last gambit. "You wrote a letter to a man named Carstens awhile back. Do you remember that?'' From the look she was giving the wall, she didn't remember where she'd put her tongue. After Buzz had kissed her and promised to stop by tomorrow, she muttered something.

"What was that, Mrs. Galloway?"

But she refused to surface from her daze.

16

To Buzz's delight we'd stopped by Kathy's office in Pioneer Square and picked her up. Wearing a long plait down the center of her back, she looked more like an actress in an Altman film than a criminal lawyer. Anybody who wanted to know could ask Buzz if she was wearing a bra. Of course, if anyone asked he'd keel over dead.

Kathy had been waxing eloquent on why the underground bus tunnel they were drilling through downtown Seattle was a boondoggle and specifically why the mayor was some sort of fascist liberal.

Buzz was all ears.

At the Steeb place I went inside with the boy. The house was empty. Kathy accompanied us, gushing over the vases and rugs. Hitler chirped, "Hide it, quick. Dad's car. Hide it, quick."

"Hide the rubbers," I said, several times, trying to teach the bird a useful phrase.

"Thomas," said Kathy, "you're incorrigible." Buzz followed her look of loving recrimination with reverence. He would have given anything to have received it.

According to a note scrawled in tight, crabby handwriting, Buzz's folks were having dinner at Victoria Station with a prospective store manager and his wife, and "Elroy" could grab a cab and join them if he got home sooner than six. It was quarter till.

Victoria Station was a block off of Lake Union smack in the middle of the city. Floatplanes routinely landed on the lake. Hundreds of sailboats and pleasure craft berthed along its shores. By boat it was a short jaunt through the Montlake Cut to Lake Washington, or, heading west, an equally scenic voyage through the government locks and out into Puget Sound. Victoria Station was a conglomeration of old railroad cars tied together and decorated with lanterns and rusty railroad paraphernalia.

A gaggle of stuffed customers came out as we were going in. The restaurant sported low ceilings and narrow passages with cramped tables. The Steebs were entertaining two younger couples.

Buzz leaned over the table and kissed his mother. A crooked-toothed lady in a red dress scooted over to make room for him. He blushed because she didn't make quite enough room to suit him, yet it was such that he couldn't avoid sitting and brushing up against her thigh. When you were fourteen, life was a pair of roller skates with a broken wheel.

Excusing himself from the group, Dudley Steeb followed Kathy and me to the front of the restaurant. He wore a natty brown suit and a yellow tie. His keys clanked at his belt. His smile was toothy enough to belong on a mule. "Evening. Find Todd?"

"Didn't Buzz tell you? We saw him last night."

"Last night? Are you serious?"

"Something spooked him, and he took off. He seemed in good health, if that's any consolation."

"I'm glad. Listen, before we go any farther, did you tell my boy heads explode when people jump from high places?"

Kathy gave me her look. I shrugged. "He asked. I told him."

"Do you think that was a wise thing to say to a fourteen-year-old boy?"

"You want me to lie?"

"I want you to keep from exciting my son's morbid curiosity. His older brother already has a fascination with suicide, may have already committed it for all we know.''

''I doubt it.''

''Mr. Black, all Buzz talked about last night was your exploits. Your private eye/cop exploits. Is it true you've killed people?'' I didn't field that one. ''I'm afraid you made too strong an impression on him.''

''I'm not in business to corrupt kids, Steeb. Today was hard on your boy. He found a dead man. Things like that need to be talked out candidly. Besides, I think you're exaggerating my effect.''

''Private detectives,'' muttered Dudley almost to himself, but not quite. Then, louder: ''I don't know what else Todd can drag us into.''

''Keep blaming Todd,'' I said, regretting my words even as they left my mouth.

''Thomas,'' hissed Kathy.

''I didn't mean to complain, Black,'' said Dudley, contrite. ''I guess I was thinking out loud.''

''Yeah, me, too. I doubt I'll be needing Buzz again anyway. I found a picture of Todd at your mother-in-law's.''

Steeb was incredulous. ''You went to the home?''

''It's a long story.''

''No, no. That's all right. In fact, I wish I'd thought of it. Rarely a week goes by that the boys don't pay her a visit. Many times they'll jog over for a couple of extra miles of training. He might show up there.''

''I don't think so. Besides, spotting him is the easy part. If he doesn't want to be cornered, we're going to need a team of cheetahs to run him to ground.''

''What did you want to see me about this evening?''

''Your brother-in-law, Jan.''

Steeb pulled his lips down over his teeth and pursed his mouth as if to kiss me, though I had a suspicion that was the last thing on his mind. His clear gray eyes never left mine.

''Jan is dead,'' Steeb said bluntly.

''What do you know about it?''

''I told Todd to leave it.''

''And?''

"He wouldn't listen."

"Why not?"

"I told Todd, and now I'm telling you. Leave it. It was just a sad thing that happened. Our family doesn't need it all churned up. Find Todd some other way."

I said, "You can answer questions or you can hire someone else. Clients do not instruct me on technique."

Steeb glanced at Kathy and then at me. He jammed his hands in his pockets and jangled some coins angrily. If anybody had asked my opinion, I would have said I was about to be fired. "Todd thinks Jan was murdered over a book Jan was supposedly writing. It's a preposterous theory. Much as we all wish he hadn't killed himself, he wasn't murdered. The police looked into it. He was despondent. He killed himself."

"What about the money?"

Giving nothing away, Steeb said, "What money?"

"The money that started America's Carpets."

"Jan had it. A loan from his mother."

"How much?"

"I don't know. It was—Hey, what is this?"

"It's all right, Dudley," said Kathy. "This will remain confidential."

Reluctantly Steeb continued. "I don't know that I ever knew the amounts. When we needed more funding, Jan went back to his mother."

"Cash? Money order? Private check? What?"

"I never really knew how it came."

"How long did that last?"

"The first couple of years. We paid it all back. Plus interest."

"Who did the bookkeeping?"

"At first Jan did. He was always good with figures. Then we hired Faith." He smiled. "I ever tell you how I won her over?"

"Swooned her?"

"I told you," he said, glumly.

"Before you two started America's Carpets, Jan worked at McCline's Towing, didn't he?"

"Coulda been."

"You know who beat your kid up three weeks ago, don't you? Four weeks ago?"

"Somebody told you about that?" Steeb's face slid as the chagrin tugged at his cheeks. He switched his gaze from me to Kathy, to his shoes. I had the suspicion he didn't have the guts to press charges. "The police said there was nothing they could do," Steeb mumbled.

"Who did it?"

"The father of his girl friend."

"A guy named McCline. Owns McCline's Towing. The same place your brother-in-law worked twenty-five years ago."

"His mother gave him the money."

"I talked to his mother. It was a scam. Jan got the money on his own and asked his mother to go along with the story that she was lending it."

"Surely you could see she is senile?" I stared at him. "She actually told you she didn't give the money?"

"She did."

"The old woman's had a stroke."

"It wouldn't take much to check into her finances at the time."

"She suffered permanent brain damage. Right after Jan died. The doctor said the stress of his death was probably a contributing factor." Steeb looked puzzled. "I don't know where he got it. I mean, if he didn't get it from his mother . . ."

"Look, I never wanted to know. Jan wasn't happy at that place. There were some rough characters used to clown around with McCline. Always getting into jams. Jan hinted at some irregular activities. I had the feeling from the way Jan acted there was something illicit about the money, but I never asked. I didn't have the faintest idea whether he was lying."

"And you paid this money back?"

"America's Carpets paid somebody back. Listen, I should know more about this, but we're talking twenty-five, twenty-eight years ago, and Jan handled the bookwork at that time.

When Elmore got into trouble with McCline, it didn't have anything to do with the past. In fact, nobody connected it up until just last week. It had to do with this girl of his. I wouldn't be surprised if he knocked her up.''

"A grown man slams your boy around? Two grown men? I would have been pissed."

"I was. I still am. The police wouldn't do anything. We tried every avenue we could think of. McCline has a brother on the force."

"That's it? McCline has a brother on the force?"

Steeb hesitated. "Faith and I discussed it. We decided . . . Look." Steeb rubbed the smile off his face with a soft, malleable hand that hadn't been visited by a callus or blister in years, fiddled with the keys at his waist, then smiled apologetically. "McCline is a hard-nosed character. I talked to him on the phone, and he said some things that put me on my guard. When I went over and saw him, I don't mind telling you I was intimidated. The man's mentally unbalanced. If Elmore behaved himself, that would be the last of it. Don't you see?"

"But Todd wouldn't behave himself?"

"With McCline? I don't know. I realize at seventeen Elmore's got a mind of his own and he's entitled to some opinions, but he is having delusions. This obsession with his uncle Jan's death. He even accused me of not wanting to pursue his trouble with McCline because I didn't want to rake up the past."

"I could accuse you of the same thing."

Steeb looked genuinely offended. "That's preposterous. It didn't have anything to do with the past. Look, Mr. Black. My brother-in-law detested McCline. McCline used to pay his employees late, cheat them on overtime, you name it. The only reason he stayed in business was he got free rent from his wife's family down in Chinatown. When he went on the skids with them, they threw him out."

"What about *The Eunuch*?"

"Another of Elmore's obsessions. I couldn't count how many times he's pored through that filthy rag."

"And Jan Galloway read *The Eunuch*?"

Exhaling loudly, Steeb said, "Yeah, sure. He seemed to be obsessed with the novel and the author, too. I don't know. Maybe this sort of insanity runs in families. Maybe it just dribbles down from the top and runs through entire generations, adopted or not. Look, I blew my top at Elmore. I guess he wasn't used to that. Normally I'm pretty even-tempered. I told him some things I'm ashamed to admit. I wish none of this had happened."

"Don't worry, Mr. Steeb," said Kathy. "Thomas will find him." I gave her a look calculated to keep the cat story from surfacing. She winked at me, then pinched my caboose on the way out of the restaurant. The girl at the cash register was grinning wickedly when I turned around to see if anybody'd spotted it. She winked, too.

17

WE TOOK LAST NIGHT'S TABLE AT THE KAU Kau, and I filled Kathy in on my day. I'd already checked Todd Steeb's hideout in the Milwaukee Hotel. Buzz had folded a rather dismal note under a tie string on the sleeping bag: "Todd, call. B." Nothing else had changed.

Kathy was all eyes, blue-violet and riveting, the exact color many young women asked optometrists to paint onto their contact lenses. When I was finished, she said, "What if Carstens didn't die by accident? What if he didn't fall into that well? What if he was pushed? That would change everything, wouldn't it?"

"Interesting premise, but it's not supported by any facts."

"Todd Steeb was out there. What if he was there when Carstens died?"

"I've been entertaining that thought all afternoon."

"And?"

Neglecting to mention the money, I said, "While Todd might have seen something, I can't cook up a reason for him to harm anybody."

"I've been reading about Clayton James all day and half the night."

"Don't forget this morning in my tub. I won't."

"Clayton James lived with his mother in San Luis Obispo until he was forty, when she died of cancer. His father ran

113

out on them when he was too young to remember, and his mother, who never remarried, became a bitter lady. She took him to England to raise him 'where they knew manners.' They came back after he graduated from Oxford.

"As far as the old lady knew, Clayton had never been on a date, never held a girl's hand. And that was just the way she wanted it. Except all this time they're living in Southern California, and Clayton's directing movies in Hollywood, and he's screwing every willing starlet who comes through the studio doors. And any whore who'll take his money. But he's making these puerile musicals and then, when the market for those falls through, light comedies: married couples with twin beds and one foot on the floor; kisses lasting less than four seconds. You remember. You're a movie junkie."

"Doris Day in tears. That cracking voice of hers." I sighed.

"And this whole time James is secretly writing *The Eunuch* at night and between movies. His mother, who must have been the queen of backstage mothers and who oversaw everything he did, knew nothing of it. She would have disowned him.

"So his mother died, and ostensibly James goes into a depression and doesn't see anyone. Only what he's really doing is polishing off his novel. It's as if the umbilical cord is finally cut. But then every publisher in New York turns it down. Several publishers offer contracts to write a Hollywood book, an autobiography or a glitzy novel, but nobody'll touch *The Eunuch*. So he sells it in France, and it begins to gain a reputation, and that reputation snowballs, and he wants to do a movie of it; but he runs into the same problem. Nobody'll touch it. Too much sex.

"Then he meets up with Delores Del Rabo, whose star has faded, and they have an affair, hot and heavy. James finally scrapes enough money together to produce the film, and he casts Delores in the lead role. Now he's made his money back a thousand times over. One of the most popular videos of all time. And Clayton James owns all the rights."

"I read somewhere he liked to gamble on the stock market."

"Terribly. They say he once lost two hundred thousand dollars in a single day."

"You always remember the book being racy," I said. "Yet, if you read it, it's more concerned with personal relationships. The priest, Rom, falls in love, and the nuns secretly murder his lover because if they don't, he'll bed her twice and be killed by the eunuchs to fulfill the Effnick law.

"So time passes, and just when Rom thinks he's as jaded as he'll ever get, he falls in love with someone who reminds him of his first love. He's trying to get some of his humanity back. He's trying to conduct what we would call a normal love affair but what, in those circumstances and under that religion, is termed sin."

"This religion has got everyone in a daze," said Kathy. "They have to reproduce. Civilization is collapsing around their heads. What appealed to men reading it was the specter of all these young things being paraded in front of the priests each night before they retired, and they get their choices, one, two, three, as many as they can handle. Wasn't that it?"

"It is quite a fantasy deal."

"And the next night it's another town and another parade of young women, all gaga over the opportunity to get impregnated by a priest. Because nobody but these priests are fertile."

We were midway through the meal, thinking about all the hoopla that had surrounded *The Eunuch* over the years, when Kathy looked out the window. It wasn't quite dusk. She rubbed a painted fingernail on her napkin. "That him?"

"Who?"

Todd Steeb stood in almost the same spot we'd seen him in last night, gazing our way, as if he suspected another ambush and chase. He had just parked his '53 Studebaker.

I went out of the restaurant through the front door and ambled up the near side of the street. He didn't make a move to flee. I don't think he recognized me. He was staring at the martial arts studio. When I drew even with him on the opposite side of the street, he suddenly recognized me. I strolled across. For a moment it looked as if he might jackrabbit.

I spoke softly, not rushing my words. "Carstens is dead."

The statement anchored him.

When I reached the sidewalk, I extended my hand to him. He surveyed either side of the street, then grasped it weakly. "Hello, Todd."

"I guess you're Mr. Black."

"Call me Thomas."

"Sure. Shit. Whatever, man."

"I want to talk. I'm not going to hold you. You want to take off after we chat, fine." I stepped back. "You already know you can outrun me. Go, if you need to."

He gave me a funny look. "Naw, that was stupid. I don't know why I ran."

"Your little brother seems to think you're scared of something."

"Shit. I've never been scared in my life. What the fuck have I got to be scared of?"

"You can tell me better than I could tell you."

His hair was the same unremarkable brown as his brother's, short and tousled. I detected a vague family resemblance around the eyes. He was small, built for endurance. The only visible remnant of McCline's beating was a mouse encircling one eye and a scabbed lip that had almost healed. The left side of his cheek was divided by three smooth welt-like scars running from the corner of his mouth to his ear. Visualizing how ugly the original wounds must have looked, I began to wonder what sorts of taunts he had suffered in school. Like his little brother, if he'd had another ounce of modesty, he'd have been invisible.

"About your uncle? About the money? Is that what you've been thinking about?"

He looked startled. "That fucking Buzz."

"Buzz has been as tight-lipped as a stone. I found out most of it on my own. I saw a brick of bills fall out of your jacket last night. Put it in my attorney's safe for you."

"I wondered what happened to those."

"They're safe."

Todd stared at me, blank-eyed, blinking. Unlike his younger brother, he was a handsome lad, scars or no. And he had something his younger brother didn't have, at least not yet: self-confidence. Todd relaxed his tense facial muscles. "I just . . . I've been in this shitty mood for weeks. Jesus H. Christ." He shook his head and let his eyes wander over the colorful signs on King Street.

"Let's put some dinner into you and see what we have to say to each other."

"Yeah. God. I'm starving. I haven't had any food all day."

In the Kau Kau I introduced Kathy, and together we ordered him a meal. We frittered away the interval between ordering and the arrival of Todd's dinner discussing pleasantries: the weather; the NBA championships; the Green River Killer. He ate with considerably more gusto than we had.

Kathy said, "Everybody's been worried."

"Yeah. Shit." His tone seemed remorseful, but the words were constructed from that brittle toughness teenagers often feign.

I said, "Your mother seems to think there's a possibility, remote, that you might have been or are considering . . . taking your own life."

Todd Steeb looked up from the pile of rice he'd been shoveling into his mouth. He chewed, swallowed, and washed it down with a gulp of hot tea, which he immediately followed with a swig of ice water. "She told you that?"

"Yeah."

"Christ. She must be worried."

" I don't think she's slept since you left. Your father either, for that matter."

"Look, Thomas. I dunno. Yeah, I guess. I wouldn't be lying to say the thought has crossed my mind. Sometimes I don't know what the fuck I'm thinking. Sometimes it all seems so empty. You know? Why not kill yourself?"

"Everybody knows that feeling," Kathy said.

"Yeah? How do you deal with it?"

Kathy was stuck for an immediate reply.

"No. Really. How do you deal with a feeling like that? That maybe things wouldn't change all that much if you were dead?"

"Love," said Kathy. "I know it sounds corny and trite,

but it fills the void. That's what it's all about. Your family loves you very much."

"I wish I could believe that."

"You have to understand it first."

Scanning her concerned face, Todd Steeb tried to come up with the next question, except there wasn't a next question. Then something clicked behind those pale gray eyes, and he assaulted the plate of rice, pork, and stir-fried green beans.

"Look," I said, "you're alone. You're scared."

"I'm not scared."

"Okay, you're alone. You're not scared. Let me be your friend." Todd didn't reply. "I don't know if you're serious about suicide or not, but I've had this conversation before, and I want to tell you about it."

"Look," said Todd, shaking his head. "Shit. I don't—"

"No, listen. I was sixteen and she was twenty-six, and she was beautiful, vivacious, owned her own business, had men falling down at her feet. She was my cousin. I'd been madly in love with her since I was two."

"Look, Thomas . . ." said Todd, his mouth full of food.

"Just listen. Because I had this conversation with her right before she killed herself."

He closed his mouth. "Yeah. Shit."

"I asked her about it because maybe I was feeling a little blue one time. And she surprised me by getting melancholy, and I could see all was not as it should have been. Later my mother said she had been having an affair with a married man, and he'd ditched her after stringing her along for two years. So we had this conversation about suicide, and it was very chatty, like ours just was, and she sounded a little bit open to it, like you just did—"

"I didn't—"

"Listen."

Todd stared at me. So did Kathy, a peculiar glint in her eye. "Sure," he said. "Go ahead. I can see you're trying to do me a fucking favor here."

"I wish somebody had said this to her. She took some pills and died about ten hours later. And it killed me, and it killed everyone in the family. It stunted me so that I was sixteen until I was twenty-one. And I was an old man, too. A thing like that breaks your life in half. Hell, you had to be there.''

"I was there, man. My uncle killed himself.''

"So he did. You want to stick a knife in your mom's heart, you want to make your dad feel a prick of guilt every day for the rest of his life—do it. You want Buzz to get so screw-brained he ends up crying every night for a year, so whacked-out he flunks out of school, gets dependent on a psychiatrist, you want to pull him down a little so he can't get any kind of jump on life, be my guest. Why not just put a gun to your little brother's head? But don't be kidding yourself that it's a decision that affects only you.

"It's going to remove a little part of everybody who loves you and a little bit of a whole bunch of people who maybe only knew you to look at you.''

Todd stared at his plate. "I don't mean anybody any harm. I'm not going to kill myself.''

"I only know what happened when my cousin died. That's all. Now forget it.'' When he finished eating, I said, "We found Carstens today. We heard you were up there this week.''

"Where'd you hear that?''

"The old man next door.''

"The police looking for me?''

"Not that I know of.''

"I got nervous . . . and I left in sort of a hurry. I found him in the well. I'd called him up about some stuff.''

"What stuff?''

"Uncle Jan did the same thing I've been doing. He went over to the James place and pretended to be a convert. Carstens knew him. Only he never knew my uncle was dead. He just knew he used to be there for Clayton's talks, and suddenly he stopped showing up. Carstens was a nice old guy.''

"What did Carstens tell you?''

"I called him up the night I ran away, and he told me he was going to do some looking around. He said he'd been suspicious for a good number of years, and when I told him about Uncle Jan being dead, it aroused more suspicions. He told me he'd found something relating to my uncle, and for me to come out to his place.''

''And?''

''He was in the well.''

''So you ran?''

''Think about it, man. I'm seventeen years old. I'm a runaway. I find a dead man in a hole in the ground. You bet I ran.''

18   "SO WHAT WERE CARSTENS'S SUSPI-
cions?" I asked.

"He was going to tell me when I got there."

"I went in the house," I said. "Know what I found?"

"You went in a dead guy's house?"

"I found a letter from somebody named Leona Galloway." Todd thought about that, but I didn't give him an
opportunity to lie. "Your grandmother. I met her with
Buzz."

He hesitated, glanced at Kathy. "She was wonderful before her stroke."

"All I found was an envelope. On the floor in the kitchen,
as if maybe it'd fallen when somebody rushed out the door."

"It wasn't me, man."

"No, you said you didn't go in. I believe you. I'm wondering what Carstens might have had. And why your grandmother would send him a letter. And why anybody would
want to steal it?"

"You ask Grandmother?"

"I did, but her picture tube was getting a little dim by the
time we got to that point. Have any idea who might have
been out to see Carstens around the time he died? Besides
you."

Todd cracked open a fortune cookie and delayed while he

121

read the ribbon of paper. He wadded it up and mortared it onto his plate, then sank his teeth into the cookie. "I got no idea who could have been there. No idea."

"Why did you run away from home?"

"Nobody told you?"

"An argument with your dad was mentioned."

"'Cause of the money. My dad found thirty thousand dollars under my bed. He wanted my head. He wanted me to stop investigating Uncle Jan's death. He even threatened to sic the cops on me. Imagine your fucking old man trying to get you to work for him for the summer for eight bucks an hour and he finds thirty grand under your bed? He about shit his pants."

"Buzz know about that money?"

"Sure."

Good old loyal Buzz. Still holding out on me, the perfect little brother. "So where'd you get it?"

"I can't say, man."

"Sure you can."

"Because it's—Look, you might want to be my friend, you might not. But I've only known you maybe thirty minutes. You think I'm going to shoot my mouth off where you can maybe find a bundle of cash, a big bundle of cash, you're crazy."

The kid still didn't know whether I had snookered him. The antibody for distrust was time, but we didn't have time. "Okay, maybe that wouldn't be too smart. Let's take it from this angle. Whose money was it?"

"I can't tell you, man."

"Got anything to do with your girl friend's father?"

He gave me a startled look, then changed the subject quickly. I let him run with the hook. "So," he said, "I guess you talked to Clayton James, too, huh?"

"I did."

"What'd you think?"

"I think egotists are generally boring."

"And his wife?"

"I had the impression there's a part of her buried under

all that makeup and posturing that you couldn't warm up with a hot coal.''

Todd Steeb laughed, then laughed some more. It was forced and loud. The other patrons in the restaurant cast wary glances his way. I didn't think it was funny enough to laugh at, but there it was. I stood up, and he stopped. Kathy shoved a tip under a teacup, and on the way to the cash register I said, ''You ready to go home?''

''I suppose.''

''And about McCline? I'd like to know why he went after you.''

''Sure,'' said Todd softly. ''Outside.''

While I chewed on a toothpick and waited for a thin Chinese man to ring up the ticket, Kathy stepped onto the sidewalk with Elmore Steeb. When I got there, Kathy was alone.

She turned her palms up at either side and gestured toward the alley with her chin. At the mouth of the alley all I could see was a running figure in the distance, blurred in the shadows. Instinctively I looked for another brick of bills, but if he'd been carrying anything, he'd have been more careful than last night.

''Shoot.''

Kathy said, ''I thought you two were getting along fairly well.''

''What'd he say?''

'' 'See ya.' Actually, it was, 'Shit, see ya, man.' You believe him, about Carstens?''

''Don't you?''

''I got the feeling he was holding back,'' said Kathy. ''And the money? Thirty thousand dollars under his bed? Give me a break.''

''Last night when I chased him a packet dropped out of his coat. You'll find an envelope in your office safe that's a hundred bucks shy of ten grand.''

She whistled. ''I stand corrected. Where did that come from?''

''Same place as the thirty. If you assume his father confiscated the thirty he found, that makes forty all told.''

''All bundled, you say? Like from a bank?''

"Uh-huh."

"Think he's got more?"

"I believe so."

"Where?"

I swept my gaze up the street, at the small groceries, restaurants, at the rock doves and panhandlers, at two brassy black hookers on the corner flirting with a sneaky-eyed businessman from Bellevue or Kirkland.

"Maybe it's in Fall City. Maybe it's in Todd's car. The only money I know about was Jan Galloway's. According to the old lady, he got a pile overnight, and it couldn't have been strictly legal. In 1959. He started the carpet business with it, and either Dudley thought Jan borrowed the money from his mother, which stretches my credulity to the breaking point, or he didn't know where he got it, or he was in on the secret. The thing is, before Jan died, he decided to go honest, to give the loot back."

"To who?"

"To whom. The joe he stole it from, I guess."

"And then he committed suicide. And then Carstens says he'll look into it for Todd, and he died."

"I keep thinking Dudley Steeb might not be too happy if Jan had decided to pull a bunch of money out of the business to pay back something that's years old and long forgotten."

I used a slim-jim on Todd's Studebaker, searched it, and found nothing except another sleeping bag with a sales slip. He'd bought it that morning at REI. Recreational Equipment Co-Op. Kathy called it Camp Yuppy. It specialized in hiking and camping gear, and there were people in Seattle who took pride in buying their clothes nowhere else. Kathy wasn't much on outdoor activities and thought the whole idea of running around town in backpacker togs was ridiculous.

Under the bag I found a lantern and digging equipment: bars, shovels, and a pick. He'd paid cash for it. My guess was he was running around with his socks full of money and still beating the bushes for more. Maybe I could race him to it. Maybe if I had the money, I would have Todd. And some answers.

We squandered two hours watching the Studebaker. He

wasn't coming back to it anytime soon. And certainly not while we were in the vicinity.

We made a couple of futile passes through Chinatown in my truck but didn't spot the kid. Kathy and I drove home to the U District, and as she was unlocking her door, she said, "How much money do you think we're talking?"

"Enough to start a business that's the envy of every rug merchant in the country. How much would that take?"

"From the things Dudley has told me, they started out with about a hundred and fifty thou. And then borrowed another hundred over the next two years."

"Jan paid off his mother's house. Who knows where else he spent it?"

"So there had to be more than a quarter of a million? Whooey."

"See you in the morning, Kathy."

She palmed my face, kissed the tip of my nose, and said, "Sleep tight."

In the morning I awakened with a start, then fetched a magnifying glass and, under a strong desk lamp, examined the envelope from Leona Galloway. The postmark was distorted, but after a session of squinting, I decided it had been mailed six years earlier, in September. The date was in double digits, but it was smudged. I phoned Faith Steeb at home and asked her without preamble when her brother had died.

"I was just getting ready for work," she replied. "Mid-September. Six years ago. Just a couple of weeks before Mother's stroke. Why? Have you found something? What?"

"Did your mother recover quickly?"

"Are you kidding? She never recovered."

"Did Jan have a lot of cash when he died?"

"He had his condo downtown and a Porsche and what he'd pumped into the business over the years. Everything was in the business."

"No safety-deposit boxes? Caribbean bank accounts?"

"Nothing. Why?"

"I'll get back to you."

Jan Galloway had died in mid-September. Shortly thereafter his mother, Leona, just before she'd suffered a near-fatal stroke, had mailed something to Carstens. Jan had been trying to give back money. Had he given it back and then committed suicide?

After driving downtown through a web of surly commuters, I went into the office and scanned my mail for the last two days, then threw some tools inside a large suitcase and had breakfast at Jenny's Deli. Afterward I drove the few blocks to Chinatown.

Somebody had found and removed my tape job on the exit door to the Milwaukee Hotel. While deliverymen were still using the back staircase, I managed to sneak upstairs into the Silver Dragon. I took a clipboard. You can go anywhere in the Western world with a clipboard. I passed through the emergency exit and into the Milwaukee Hotel without being noticed.

I started with McCline's old towing company offices but spent only an hour and a half there. I pulled up floorboards and went through the plaster and lathe of one wall. Tapping along the other walls produced only the proper tones.

The basement was the place.

My unfair advantage was that Todd's younger brother had already told me Todd knew this part of the block much better than he did. Todd had been exploring these catacombs.

It didn't take me long to uncover evidence of Todd's search. Yet it wasn't until some thirteen hours had passed, and I had already surfaced once for fresh nine-volt batteries, that I started getting ruthless. I even ripped into part of the wall that butted up against the basement of the Chinese gambling club, then patched it before they showed for their afternoon mah-jongg. I returned to the secret passage Buzz Steeb had shown me, the one with the six small rooms. I knew a little about construction, and I tried to calculate where extra passages might be cut through the walls.

It went clean under the street.

That's what fooled me. I'd been taking it for granted that the painted concrete basement walls in the front of the building couldn't possibly lead anywhere. But tapping with a crowbar over every inch of every wall in the forward passage had produced hollow wooden sounds on the side facing the street, on a section I had mistakenly thought to be solid.

Ever the subtle one, I used a pick-head ax on the panel, splintering the wood until a cool draft kissed my perspiring face. If there had been a secret button, I had crushed it.

Five minutes later I was staring into a small one-man tunnel which led directly under King Street. It smelled musty, and I had to crouch to use it. A small man or woman could probably walk upright.

Using a strong lantern and listening to the trucks thunder overhead, I crossed under the street. The passageway led to a cramped, dingy basement on the south side of King Street. A single wooden staircase led upstairs into the building. I followed it up two flights, smelling raw dough from a bakery in the building. The stairs led to an abandoned apartment building above the street-side shops. Looking out through a cracked windowpane, I could see the faded facade of the Milwaukee across the street. At the east corner of the building hung the gaudy sign for the Silver Dragon.

It didn't take me long to pick up trails in the rat raisins and sheets of dust. An hour later I located a false floor in a closet. He hadn't replaced the lid as neatly as he might have, had left a fresh splinter to be caught in the gleam of my flashlight.

When I speared the top of the panel with my ax and lifted it off, two large gunnysacks were lodged in the hole.

Neither was tied. They were marked "McCline Towing" in frazzled black ink.

On the lookout for booby traps I used the end of my crowbar to open the neck of the largest sack.

Greenbacks.

Hundreds of them.

19

FOR THIRTEEN HOURS I'D BEEN SWINGing crowbars and pickaxes, and now the trove I'd uncovered erased any doubts in my mind that six years before Jan Galloway had been murdered.

I was staring at the cause.

All hundreds, there were a hundred of the critters in each banded packet, same as the one Todd had dropped last night. I piled the contents of the first sack five high and ten across. The stacks were equal and squared off; they hadn't been manhandled enough to mar their banker's corners. The second sack contained three hundred thousand.

Total: eight hundred grand.

Plus three bricks that Dudley Steeb had confiscated. And one I'd found in the alley. Another forty thousand.

Todd must have been the one who'd replaced the floorboard and left the white of a splinter showing like a blond hair on a black wool shirt. If the kid had any brains, he would have secured the bundles in a safety-deposit box. Anybody could make off with this. To think nothing of other calamities. The entire block was a fire trap.

Thirty minutes later I was home, peering at my face in the bathroom mirror, scrubbing my hands, and screwing a washrag into my ears. I brushed my hair and changed my shirt. It was almost nine-thirty. I hadn't seen a newspaper or listened to the radio all day. I felt as if I'd just gotten back from a night trip to Iowa. When I fetched the *Times* off the front porch and caught the remnants of a violet and striated ocher sunset, it didn't interest me.

I wandered to the interior basement door to Kathy's apartment and knocked. No answer. I tramped out into the backyard and clipped a few roses, a Troika and some Snowfires, trimmed them, and put them into a vase.

Using my key, I descended the interior stairs to Kathy's apartment. It was dark. I surveyed her bathroom for a minute, trying to visualize how best to gut and enlarge it. Her clown makeup was on the vanity and the black-and-white mime's suit hanging nearby. She was trying to establish her criminal law business on a small inheritance from a distant aunt, and she felt she might operate marginally for a year, possibly two, provided she had cheap rent.

These days she no longer told me about her men. My affair with Judy Banner had put a crimp on our date talk.

Judges, lawyers, corporate executives—they all were intrigued with Kathy Birchfield, attorney-at-law. But she wasn't snooty. For three weeks she'd kept company with a cabdriver who painted cityscapes in his down time. She didn't date many twice. It was a trait she shared with me, for prior to Judy Banner I'd been celibate a year.

It wasn't my money. It never would be. It had been Jan Galloway's, and even he had swiped it, or found it, or swindled it. Where else would a tow truck driver get eight hundred grand?

I dialed my answer machine at the office. Henry Ritzmo, a paunchy, elderly businessman who ran a jewelry store in Pioneer Square and had the sort of contagious bellowing laughter that made everyone within earshot want to join in, wanted me to escort him tomorrow when he took the cash from his safe and carried it to his bank. He paid ten dollars for the trip, but I did it as a favor, toting a plastic .45 squirt gun so he could see the butt in my pocket. He was fond of asking tongue-in-cheek questions such as "How many bad guys you generally arrest per day?" One a day, I said. My quota was one per day.

Dropping onto the sofa in the living room, I picked up the phone, dialed Judy Banner, and waited for her husky voice. She wasn't in. I dialed the home on Capitol Hill.

As always she answered on the second ring, never the first. Never the third or fourth. "Judy."

"Thomas. How nice of you to call."

"Something wrong?"

"Nothing, Thomas. I just said—"

"I can hear it in your voice. Something's wrong."

"You've been a shamus too long. You're paranoid. You want to see me?"

"When are you free?"

"Actually, not until later in the week. Marcella came down with a bug and hasn't been in."

"You have time to talk?"

"Thomas, I wish I did. I've got Moyer in the tub, and I need to keep an eye on him."

"Later then. I love you, Judy."

"Love you, too, Thomas."

Weepy Moyer was a young man with a degenerative nerve disease that had turned him into something children stared at. He wore a baseball helmet, walked, no, waddled, haltingly with the aid of leg braces and crutches, and was addicted to computer games. Once when Weepy choked on an apple, Judy slapped his back and urged him to spit a piece of the slobbered-up fruit directly into her cupped hand. Before I saw her do it, I thought only mothers had that much devotion.

Still in her robe, face pulled taut by a damp towel worn turban fashion on her head, Kathy stood over my bed, gawking at my naked chest and the tops of my pajama bottoms.

I gripped a pistol, my favorite .45 automatic, tuned as tightly as a target gun, yet not so tightly as to corrupt its integrity, and accepting hard balls instead of wadcutters.

Pointed at her nose.

"Well, squeeze me," she said, turning pale.

I blinked, finished waking up, and dropped the gun to the mattress. "Todd show up yesterday?"

"Not a peep."

"Where were you last night?"

"Where were you all day, buster? I hadda take a bus to work. You know my car's on the fritz." I could tell from the rings under her eyes she'd been out late. "What's the gun about, Cisco?"

Using my left hand, I reached under the bed and flung the sacks at her feet. She stooped and unknotted the tie strings. "Holy Moses."

"My thoughts exactly."

"Is it real?"

"I've had a couple of classes on counterfeiting. They're all good."

As soon as the banks opened, Kathy and I escorted Henry Ritzmo to his savings and loan with seventeen hundred dollars, crumpled fives, tens, and twenties, in a satchel. I wore my blued automatic in a shoulder holster, having left the squirt pistol in a drawer in Kathy's office. Kathy lugged a suitcase containing almost a million dollars in hundreds. Outside his destination Ritzmo squinted at me in the sunshine and patted his side pocket, then, with a malevolent smile, hefted a plastic squirt gun of his own.

"Got me a heater," he said, bursting into jolly laughter.

"Nice work, Henry." I winged my jacket open. Glimpsing the .45, he laughed all the harder, thinking it was still plastic.

Kathy and I leased a set of safety-deposit boxes at a bank near her building. From my tiny back room in Kathy's offices, I phoned Clayton James. This whole thing had blown up from a simple runaway to something I didn't have a handle on. All anybody was asking was the return of Todd Steeb, but I knew I'd probably never nab him unless I learned the details of his investigation, unless I found out where the money belonged. I was thinking James might be able to put a finger on the connection between the money and Jan Galloway. Also, we needed to talk about Carstens. No answer.

I drove home to the U District, changed into a pair of black riding shorts and a bright red jersey, climbed onto my Miyata and pedaled to Renton and back, via the Arboretum. Almost thirty miles in the late May sunshine. I rode a low gear, spinning, and it took an hour and twenty minutes. Afterward I spent some time lifting weights in my spare bedroom. The first summer heat rode a slight breeze through the windows.

After a quick shower I dialed the Steeb household. Voice croaking, a young man answered.

"Yo?" I could hear Hitler jabbering in the background.

"Buzz?"

It took a moment for the line to go dead.

It wasn't Buzz.

Knowing his younger brother would be in school, and mom and dad at work, Todd had sneaked home, probably for fresh socks and Flintstone vitamins. Maybe for cash. After all, I'd confiscated almost ten grand from him two days ago. But why wouldn't he go to his stash in Chinatown? Maybe he had.

When I clambered into the Ford and drove to the Steeb place in Mount Baker, the house was locked, although I could hear Hitler screeching inside.

Two houses away an old woman slow-dancing with a rake confirmed he'd raced off five minutes earlier.

I had a brunch at the Tai Tung across the street from the Kau Kau, gobbling hombows and scarfing tea at the café counter, then walked across King to the sad old hotel. I sauntered around the base of the building. A boarded-up door in the back of the Milwaukee off the alley was propped open with half a brick. You had to look twice to see it. Using a small high-intensity flashlight I'd been carrying, I made my way inside and climbed a pitch-dark flight of stairs to the first floor of the Milwaukee.

Despite the dismal environs, the sunlight angling in through the open apartment doors gave the place a cheery aspect. It stopped being cheery when I got to the room where Todd Steeb had stashed his gear. It was topsy-turvy. *The Eunuch* had been ripped in half.

Using my space-age flashlight, I worked my way to the basement and tried to judge whether anybody had traipsed through after I'd exhumed the money. I'd left a large broken crate blocking the tunnel entrance. It appeared undisturbed.

I went through the rooms and then the tunnel, crossed under the street, and spent twenty minutes wandering around the vacant upstairs, listening to business being transacted in the shops below.

Searching for traces of whoever had rifled Todd Steeb's belongings, I crawled back through the basement and made a grid-by-grid trek through the Milwaukee. It could have been a bum. It could have been a snoopy caretaker. A waiter from the Silver Dragon looking for a place to smoke dope. A cop on patrol.

I had wandered all the way to the fourth floor, picking my way through pigeon guano, when I drifted into a vacant apartment and peeked out a window at the interior air well.

Thirty seconds elapsed before I saw him.

At the bottom of the air shaft a disjointed man in khaki trousers and a leather jacket was sprawled on his face.

I shouted, but he didn't move.

20 When I reached him, I said, "Todd?"

Gently I laid two fingers against his carotid artery. He was warm, but I felt no pulse. I suctioned my ear against his back, trying to hear a heartbeat. I heard gurgling, but you could hear gurgling sticking your ear alongside a can of beer. I palpated his cervical vertebrae and felt a lump of emotion forming in my gut.

His neck was badly broken. The fall had smashed his face, but not as badly as you would think.

Dead.

Before the police came, sitting alone at the bottom of the air shaft in the broken glass and dried leaves and bits of faded newspaper and pigeon feathers, I made repeated and unsuccessful efforts to inhale deeply. Todd and I had been playing a game of sorts, and now some unknown kibitzer had interfered. I felt a hot tear streak down my cheek.

I looked up. Three stories to the roof.

I sat in the windless well, listening to the cooing of a pigeon as it strutted along the roofline, to the scratch of its feet on the tin rain gutter. Todd was still warm. I might have called the cops then, but I think I was in shock.

Upstairs on the flat tar roof trying to calculate how he'd gone off, I discovered a note wedged into a crevice.

On a blank three-by-five card, scribbled half in cursive and half in block printing, were the penciled words "I'm too sorry—Elmore." Too sorry? Strange phrase. I left the card.

A waitress in the Silver Dragon let me use the phone, and as I did so, I noticed my hands were shaking. Two minutes later I ushered the first blue-and-white officers in. I might have told them I was retired from the SPD, but I didn't feel like engaging in the idle chitchat this revelation would ignite. I had a gnawing fear Todd had committed suicide, in part, because he had discovered someone had pilfered his money. I was still assuming it had been his stash. I had been delinquent in not leaving a note.

He must have figured some whacked-out dehorn was squandering it on two-thousand-a-night hotel rooms and cases of Thunderbird.

You could see the Kingdome and all of downtown Seattle from the top of the Milwaukee. I stared mindlessly at the skyline while a sergeant and a balding policeman inspected the note and discussed the dead boy in tones that were a perfect synthesis of boredom and reverence.

Finally I interrupted. "The note's a fake."

"Pardon me?" said the sergeant, a young Asian, unsure of himself, book smart and street-shy.

"For one thing, it's too short. He would have written twenty pages. The kid had a lot on his mind. I gave him a talk about suicide last night."

The cops swapped dubious glances. The sergeant said, "You got training as a counselor?"

"No."

"Uh-huh," said the sergeant without buying a word of it.

I decided it was futile. I could tell them about Carstens—two falling deaths in one week—I could tell them about Todd's uncle dying from the same roof here at the Milwaukee, I could tell them that he had gone by Todd, not Elmore, but I had been a cop long enough to know I was the only Indian who was going to make a difference. They would file away their reports, and then the medical examiner would file away the boy, and then the friends and relatives would file away their memories and their black suits and long faces. Everybody would forget.

Jan Galloway. Carstens. And now Todd.

The air was thick with suicides, accidents, coincidences. Men were dropping from the sky everywhere you looked.

We were downstairs again when the sergeant said, "You think this was murder, we'll investigate it as a suspicious death." He handed me his card. His name was Koba. "Give me a call in a day or two."

I thanked him halfheartedly and wandered out onto the street in the sunshine, dazed, defeated, and curiously dishonored.

I'd had him. The night before last I'd had Todd "Elmore" Steeb in my grasp. Right here on King Street.

I found Kathy with a client and waited in the anteroom, mindlessly scanning a copy of *People* magazine. I perused an entire article on Princess Di as if I cared. I kept thinking about Todd defending his little brother from a pair of attack dogs. I kept trying to remember when I'd ever known a kid with that sort of courage.

As I told Kathy about it, I kept picturing the odd angle of Todd's running shoes on his feet, akimbo from the fall. I kept thinking about that hot leather jacket and what a warm day it was. About those fine, smooth fingers that would never caress another keyboard. About whoever had gone through his belongings.

Despite what I told the police, I wasn't sure if he'd jumped or been pushed. I'd located an open stairwell leading directly to the roof. But who would be on the roof of the Milwaukee Hotel with a seventeen-year-old runaway?

When I finished, Kathy thumbed her intercom. "Beulah, cancel my appointments for the rest of the day."

"Stay and work," I said. "It'll help you forget."

"I want to be with you when you tell Buzz."

"What makes you think the police haven't already contacted his family?"

"Because I know you. You sent the police to Dudley and Faith at their offices. You're telling the boy yourself."

He was home, answered the front door with his clarinet

in hand. He exposed that fan of separated teeth, then blushed when he saw Kathy in the truck. His thick eyebrows raised involuntarily. He'd shaved and given himself a shaver burn doing it. I was frantically trying to figure a way to say what I had to say that wouldn't be too blunt, too roundabout, or too doctrinaire. I knew it was best if it was candid and quick. The words I was about to let fly would stick in this boy's craw the rest of his life. I kept thinking about the night my father pulled me out of a pickup basketball game to tell me my cousin was dead. It seemed like three minutes ago.

I knew from experience that the more pussyfooting and delay, the more Buzz would resent me. It had to be gentle and direct.

"We need to talk, guy."

"Sure, Thomas. Come on in, man. I was just fixing to practice."

"Your parents call?"

"My folks?"

"I hate like hell to be the one telling you this, but I feel like I owe you."

"Sure. What?"

I paused. "We found Todd this afternoon. He'd fallen. He passed on, Buzz."

The fourteen-year-old boy in front of me didn't say a word. He gulped. Blinked. Fingered the keys on his clarinet absentmindedly. The wet, wooden sound of their clicking was the only disturbance in the room until Hitler said, "Am I pretty?" The bird repeated the question. Buzz walked to the living-room window in that bowlegged walk of his and looked out at nothing.

"I don't know where Hitler got that. I didn't teach it to him," he said finally. "I mean, nobody around here is pretty, especially that bird."

"Girls and beer," said the bird.

"I taught him that. Me and Todd. Todd loved that old parrot. Used to teach him the nastiest words he knew. Mom would spend about a week trying to unteach them."

"I'm sorry," I said. "There's nothing else I can say. I'm sorry."

"He called last night," said Buzz. "Said I finked on him."

"I told him you didn't."

"Only he didn't believe you. Dad heard me on the phone and picked up the extension in his den, but Todd hung up." Buzz blinked back his first tear. "How did it happen?"

"In Chinatown. At the Milwaukee. I think he had a dizzy spell or something. Fell from the roof. Must have been up there trying to figure how your uncle Jan bought it.

Buzz spoke softly. "Todd never had dizzy spells. He was an athlete."

"Okay, well, I might as well say it. The cops are going to want to say he jumped."

"He did it? He went and killed himself?"

"That's the way it looked. I don't believe it. And I know you don't." Choosing my words with exquisite and painful care, I told him how and where I found his brother. He listened without meeting my eyes.

When I was through, he said, "Maybe I better be by myself."

"You going to be okay?"

"Sure, why wouldn't I?"

"Let me stick around, and we'll talk."

"I'm all right."

When I got outside on the front porch, I looked out over Lake Washington at the dim, dingy green foothills to the east. My feet seemed rooted to the wooden deck. Summer was beginning. It was time to get out to the Snoqualmie Valley and pedal my bike. Even from here I could see the heat waves on the East Side. Inside the house a series of clarinet scales began. Ordered. Precise. I listened to them for two minutes before they gradually deteriorated into a muddle and ceased.

As I headed down the front steps, Faith Steeb parked her new BMW on the street. Looking drawn and about ten pounds skinnier, she climbed the stairs breathlessly. Hollows under her eyes. Mourning fit her personality like a glove. She had been born to grieve, the way some people had been born to pitch baseballs. I could see now any smiling she'd done in her life had been under protest.

"Mr. Black?"

"I wanted to be the one."

"I guess I should thank you for that. I wasn't looking forward to it." I peered over her shoulder at the street. "They tell me you found our boy. But it was only three stories he fell? I didn't think a thing like that—"

"A fall from a barstool can kill you."

"I suppose. Did he—"

"Suffer? It was just like that."

"Twice in one family. It's too much."

"The police tell you it was a suicide?"

"No, but of course, it was."

"Sometimes they run in families," I said. "It's like one inspires the other. Like a contagion. But I don't think that's what happened."

"Of course it is."

I watched her get out her keys and fiddle with the front door. She tried three separate keys before she stabbed the correct one into the lock.

Five minutes later as we pulled in front of Sonja McCline's house, Kathy said, "What's this?"

"Todd's girl friend."

"Can't you just let her—"

"Hear it from Jean Enersen on the five o'clock news?"

Bubbly as ever, Sonja met me at the door. I went inside. Thirty minutes later I fired up the engine and made tracks.

"Pretty girl," said Kathy. "Her father's the one who beat up Todd?"

"Him and his drinking buddy."

"He came through the yard when you were in there. Her father. Gave me the willies. But I've been out here thinking. You didn't tell the police about the money, did you?"

"I want it to be a lure."

"What if we never locate the rightful owner?"

"As my mother would say, tough titty."

We supped at a Vietnamese restaurant at Twelfth and Jackson. We were the only non-Asians in the joint. It seemed all I was doing these days was eating, sleeping, finding cash, and looking at corpses. By tacit agreement, we talked about everything except Elmore Steeb and the case. Afterward I drove to West Seattle. It seemed best to keep moving.

21

CLAYTON JAMES WAS AS NATTY AS ever. His living room was steamy with the body heat of young women and bearded young men, university types all, crowding on the low furniture or squatting cross-legged on the rug. Nobody in the house had ever listened to a radio station that played ads for drag races. They all made regular donations to Greenpeace and never reneged on their public television pledges. Maybe I was misjudging, but most of them looked like the sort who'd had "nervous breakdowns" a week before graduating from college.

"Come in," urged James, stroking his thin mustache and eyeballing Kathy. He smiled thinly. "Come in. Don't by shy. I'm always happy to see new faces."

"James, I need to talk to you. It's personal."

He smiled a beatific smile and glanced around the group, soaking up the adoration. It was the sort of celebrity worship that corrupts. "Certainly, we can talk here in front of these"—he smiled—"young apostles of cinema."

"You want to talk here?"

"Why not?"

"Your gardener is dead."

The group gasped as one. Most of them had been acquainted with the old man. Genuinely shocked, Clayton James bobbled his eyebrows. His cheeks drooped, and for

141

an instant he looked like a man with something less than 150 pounds of ego pressurized in a 10-pound persona. "Carstens? How on earth? Carstens?"

"The King County police said they were going to call you. I guess they got swamped handing out traffic tickets."

"Carstens was getting on in years, but he seemed in fine health."

"Fell into his well."

Clad in a long black caftan inset with colorful pearls and beads, reds, yellows, and maroons, Delores came out of the kitchen in open-toed high heels and said, "Darling. I forgot to tell you. Some policeman did call about Carstens."

She moved like a spry forty instead of a bedridden sixty-three. Speed, steroids, blood transfusions, and who knows what else.

"God, Delores . . ." Clayton said, anguish racking his voice. It was the first thing I'd ever heard him utter that might not have come from an automaton. "How on earth could you overlook something like that?"

She gave him a rueful look. "I didn't want to disturb you, dear."

"I see."

Even on her spiked heels the stoop-shouldered woman moved quickly and stealthily, almost like a cat. On my first visit I would have sworn she was bedridden, yet now she didn't so much as limp. We all had our good days and bad days, but for her the pendulum swung farther than most.

"Todd Steeb is dead, too," I said. "They found his body in a building in the International District. The police think he committed suicide. They're investigating." There was a general commotion among James's guests in response to my second announcement.

"Unbelievable," said Clayton James, perching near the fireplace mantel next to an ashtray and an assortment of pipe fixings.

"That dear, sweet boy?" said Delores James. "Surely you're mistaken?"

"No mistake. Mind if I ask a question or two? Carstens

was helping the boy with something. Either of you have an idea what it was?''

"Carstens and the young man talked at great length," said Clayton James. "As far as a project goes, I can't think of one. Can you, Delores?''

She shook her head.

I said, "Doesn't it surprise you that he committed suicide?''

"Not really," said James. "I guess he's just chosen another path. We shall miss his joy. His inquisitive mind. Let us all bow our heads for a silent memory and prayer.''

After many moments of silence James said, "Fara, fara, Taraway. Young one rest in peace. The last to arrive is sometimes the first to leave. Fara, fara, Taraway." If was from his novel, a pray in the Effnick religion. I couldn't remember the rest of it, but a young woman with huge breasts sitting cross-legged on the floor mumbled parts of it under her breath. A man in wire-rimmed glasses and muttonchop whiskers next to her nodded in agreement. I had the feeling everyone in the room except Kathy and me knew the novel by heart.

Delores hoisted a sculptured metal goblet to her lips and sipped delicately.

"Either of you remember Jan Galloway? Six years ago? He might have been writing a book about you, Clayton. He used to show up at these soirees." After I had described him to the best of my ability, they shook their heads in concert. "Either of you seen Todd Steeb since the last time I was here?" Negative. "Anybody in the room seen Todd Steeb this week anywhere except in this house?" Nobody had. I plunged ahead. "Was Carstens doing anything out of the ordinary during the last week?''

"No," said Delores. "Carstens never did anything out of the ordinary.''

"True," said Clayton James, tamping a wad of tobacco into the pipe bowl with his thumb. "We'll miss him, but he *was* boring.''

"Mind if I look through his things?''

"Not at all," said Delores. Unexpectedly she led us

through the house, out the back door, and down a paved walkway to a small aluminum-walled toolshed in the garden. She moved at a brisk canter. The air in the shed was stifling from the heat of the day, though it was now bathed in shade from a grape arbor.

"Nice place," said Kathy, admiring the view of the sound and then the fading blossoms on a bank of purple azaleas.

"Thank you," said Delores. Her toenails were painted vermilion. She opened the unlocked shed and swung the door wide, flipped a light switch, and then picked up a loose sickle on a stool and buried it in a wooden post.

"Neat trick," I said.

"Grew up on a farm in Michigan. Until I was sixteen and ran away, I did everything. Slaughtered pigs, raised ducks, milked cows. Ran a tractor. You name it. I've outlived all my brothers."

Carstens hadn't left much. It took all of three minutes for me to examine two changes of clothing, a book of crossword puzzles, a locker containing cheese and crackers, and a small refrigerator. There was a shelf of gardening and plant books. Delores stood in the doorway, giving Kathy a look that resembled the beady-eyed gaze I'd once seen a golden eagle at the zoo giving a leashed chihuahua. But then, Kathy got that look from a lot of women.

Before we exited out the side gate, I said, "Were you and Clayton married in 1959?"

"Honeymooned in Mexico. It was the year I shot my last Hollywood film."

"And when did you start shooting *The Eunuch*?"

"Shame on you. Don't you know? It was early '60 when we began *The Eunuch*. After my accident. I filmed some of my close-ups in a wheelchair. But there's something— If you don't mind answering a question yourself, Mr. Black. When you mentioned Todd Steeb's death, you said the police were taking care of it. Surely, in the event of a suicide. . . ?"

"They're investigating it as a suspicious death," I said.

"Why on earth would they do that?"

"I talked them into it."

"You?"

"Things didn't look kosher."

"What things?"

"Nothing important. Clayton been around all day?"

"He's been out riding around on that miserable wheel of his. I don't know why he rides it. To get out of the house, I suspect."

"Was there any money missing from that movie?"

"What do you mean?" Delores flung the remnants of her drink onto a cactus plant. The meat on her arm was surprisingly firm as she air-dried the goblet with a curt, waggling motion.

"There might be a rather large sum of money in Chinatown, hidden. I'm just wondering where it belongs."

She made a gesture with her lower lip that said she didn't know and didn't care. The move dismissed us at the same time. I bade her good-bye, but she'd already pivoted and was headed vigorously back to the house.

"She looks wonderful," said Kathy.

"If you don't notice the stitch marks."

"In a kind of a Halloweeny way." She giggled. "Aren't we catty? Actually, when she was younger, she looked a bit like Lana Turner. I thought you said she was an invalid."

"I thought she was."

"She's how old?"

"Early sixties."

"They'll have a new gardener by Monday," said Kathy.

"Probably already hired one."

22

I BLEW HALF A DAY SHOWING TODD'S picture to bums, shopkeepers, clerks, streetwalkers, and truck drivers who frequented Chinatown. Two people recognized the photo. The first said he was their paper boy. The second said the photo was one of his wife's relatives who lived in Hawaii. Several people recalled his car, which the police had found five blocks away, but nobody recalled him. So much for eyewitnesses.

From a Filipino gentleman who was almost four and a half feet tall and who pretended not to understand a word of English, I managed to rent a shabby unused room across the street from the Milwaukee. Sign language and pidgin English didn't do a thing for the little man. Cash became our Esperanto. The room presented an unblocked view of most of the Milwaukee's street-side windows, the alley entrance, and the exit on King Street.

I hired Bridget Simes, a winsome detective of long acquaintance, to share twelve-hour shifts watching the Milwaukee. We secreted a microphone in McCline's old offices. I showed Bridget pictures or gave elaborate written descriptions of all the principals: both elder Steebs, Buzz, Clayton James and his wife, Sonja, McCline, and Scotty Fogle. Each of us kept a camera handy with a 135-millimeter lens and high-speed black-and-white film. Cockroaches decorated the walls like bullet holes in a country stop sign, but the room had a phone, an AM radio, a bathroom, and a kitchenette.

Planning to reimburse myself from the eight hundred grand when and if I settled things, I paid Bridget from my own account. I couldn't let this drop. Todd had been murdered, and somebody who should have been sleeping in a steel bunk wasn't.

After penning a lengthy report, I had it delivered to the Steebs. I salted the document with hints that some money might be lying loose near Todd's death site. I wanted as many people as possible mulling it over. To most it would be a wild-cat rumor. To those who knew something, either through Todd or his uncle six years earlier, it might be a poisoned carrot.

When I wasn't staking out the Milwaukee and McCline's old offices, I did some hectic research into the months of October, November, and December of 1959 in the Seattle-Tacoma area, rooting around for an unsolved robbery, an embezzlement, a jewel heist, a series of robberies, or some other mysterious happening that might account for Jan Galloway's sudden wealth. An armored car had been ripped off near Everett, but the cash and bonds had been recovered, the bandits incarcerated.

I learned who owned all the relevant properties in Chinatown from 1959 until the present. None of it intertwined with anything else I'd run across. McCline's late wife's family had owned most of the block, though they had given up their holdings shortly after evicting McCline. Across the street the abandoned apartments where I'd located the money had gone through a succession of owners. I couldn't discern anything from the names. A friend conversant with the history of Chinatown went over my findings, but she had nothing to add.

Two days after Todd's death I phoned Sergeant Koba. He referred me to a Detective Brown. Sounding young and polite, his raw-hamburger voice that of an inveterate smoker, Brown was succinct.

"Suicide, Black. That's what it boils down to. He died of a broken neck, but the skull injury alone would have killed him. You don't fall three stories and land on your head and then get up and ask for a Tootsie Roll. His younger brother tried to tell us it wasn't his handwriting on the note, but we can't prove that. Our experts says he might have written it. He was upset. Fits all the patterns: runaway, trouble at home, at school. This was his second-go-round.''

"Second time he ran away?''

"Didn't his folks clue you in? A year ago he garaged that old car of his and left the motor running. He was so rummy afterward he never could tell anyone whether he'd done it on purpose. His parents have been keeping a close eye on him ever since. Including hiring you.''

"So that's it, huh?''

"Why? You got something to add?''

I thought it over. They could trace the bills I'd found, but I'd already had an old friend who worked for Alcohol, Tobacco, and Firearms run checks. Except that most of them were twenty-eight years old and uncirculated, nothing about them was noteworthy. Two hundred and fifty grand was newer. Late seventies issues. My guess was Jan Galloway had kept his stash intact, spending only what was necessary. The newer bills had come from his repayments.

"Nothing to add. Thanks.''

"Think nothing of it.''

As I sat in a straight-backed chair in the stale apartment in Chinatown, rereading Todd's torn copy of *The Eunuch* and watching the Milwaukee, I couldn't help reliving some of my own high school days. Certain things had seemed so important at the time, yet from this perspective they looked no worse than trifling. Kids look at life from the wrong end of the telescope.

I'd been an outsider all my life, but I was a piker compared with Todd Steeb. He was the outsider's outsider. He'd wanted to be a spy, the maverick wanting to fit into a job that kept him on the periphery. I guessed the same impulse had pushed me into investigations after I got pensioned off from the SPD, that feeling of alienation, of being lonely in a crowd, of wanting to work on your own. He'd felt so alienated he'd even destroyed all his own pictures.

The funeral was scheduled for Monday at one o'clock. I

wasn't looking forward to it. I hated rituals, and few rituals
made me more uncomfortable than funerals.

Shortly before nine Sunday evening I got a call from
Bridget. "Noises," she said, "coming across our micro-
phone. In the old McCline Towing offices. Two of them.
Sounds like a woman and a man."

"Been there long?"

"Just this minute."

"Dehorns, or what?"

"I can't tell."

Slender, well-trained, and ruthless when she had to be,
Bridget could take care of herself. She met me at Maynard
Alley and King.

"Still inside?" I asked.

"The alley door is still open."

"Stick around and see if I flush 'em. The front door dumps
onto the street. If you stay here at the corner, you can watch
both exits."

"What if I see somebody running out here with your wallet and toupee?"

"Hey," I said, grinning, "this is the real deal." I tipped
my head. "Yank."

"I'll yank it when I have time to do it right." She laughed
thinly. "Serious. You want me to call the police if you don't
show?"

"Play it by ear, hon."

She nodded.

Using a five-cell flashlight with a hankie over it, I had got
all the way down the inside stairwell, only twenty feet from
the door to the McCline Towing offices, when the whispering
in the offices stopped precipitously. The creaky stairs were
as noisy as baseball cleats in a library.

They'd made me. More whispering. I didn't recognize either voice.

I clicked off the flashlight, stopped, breathed softly through
my mouth, and waited forty seconds before the revolver came
around the corner. I moved forward on the creaky floorboards until I was one quick jump from the gun.

The barrel of the weapon edged farther out. A shadowy

chunk of a blond head came after it. The head was steady. The gun was quivering.

Snapping my flashlight on and holding it high, I said, "Empty your hands or start shooting. Your choice." The gun stopped shaking. It disappeared momentarily, then flew into the hallway.

A moment later a blond kid of about eighteen stepped out, husky and so scared his blue eyes looked like fifty-cent pieces. He wore a green and black letterman's jacket from Franklin and showed his palms at eye level. The woman wore garish red-brown hair in a blunt China Chop and had enough pale white makeup on her face for a zombie. All her clothing was jet black.

"Sonja," I said.

Frozen, the boy spoke to Sonja. "Who's this?"

"He's the one I told you about. The private detective."

Standing upright, the boy said, "You really seen heads explode?"

"Not lately. Whose gun?"

"My father's," he said, smiling warily. "I borrowed it. Thirty-eight police special."

"Loaded?"

"Sure."

"I know people who would have shot you loose of it before they said a word." I scuffed it over with my foot, flipped open the cylinder, clunked six bullets onto the floor, then handed it to him by the open frame. "Put it back in your father's sock drawer next to his bolo ties. What are you doing here?"

The blond youth looked pleadingly to Sonja for an answer. Sonja glowered stubbornly. "What's it to you?"

"What's your name?" I asked the boy.

"Robert Hendrickson. She wanted me here, you know? Scared to come alone. I don't know what we're doing. She started messing with the walls and shit. Using that crowbar."

"Wait outside. Take that flashlight, and give it to the pretty lady in the raincoat standing at the alley. Sonja'll be out in a minute." He took the stairs out.

When we were alone, I stepped up to her and swept Sonja's

face with the beam of the flashlight. Fumes of alcohol wafted on her breath. The white powder on her face in the puny light of my flashlight made her look like death itself. I reached out and touched her cheek. She flinched, squinted hard against my hand. I rubbed gently.

I brushed a swatch of makeup off to reveal a black eye. "Somebody beat you."

She looked down at her black high tops. I thought she was going to cry, but she was tougher than that, only swallowed and bit her lip and let her blocky shoulders sag. "He wanted to find out about Todd. After Todd died, it was like . . . I dunno. Dad went weird on me. I told him some things he shouldn't know."

"Like what?"

"About Todd finding all that money."

"You knew about that?"

"Me and Buzz know. Yeah."

"So how much did he find?"

"He wouldn't say, but I knew it must be close to fifty thousand. He said he thought it had been hidden since way before we were born. He had four packages of ten thousand each. Did you know that?"

"Dudley got three of them. I confiscated the other. What'd your father ask?"

"I told him forty thousand. It set him off. He went ditsy."

"Did he know about it already?"

"I dunno. We were talking about Todd's being dead and all, and Dad mentioned the ring Todd gave me and said wasn't that something, a kid that age having a ring worth five grand. I said . . . I don't remember what I said. Then all of a sudden Dad was punching me."

"He do that often?"

"Last time was about a year ago. He won't hit me if he isn't drunk."

"Drunk as an excuse went out with horse biscuits in the streets. What else did he want to know?"

"He seemed to know about Mr. Galloway, Todd's dead uncle. I don't know how he knew."

"Galloway used to work for your dad."

She looked shocked. ''Nobody ever told me that.''

''What'd he ask about Todd's uncle?''

''If Todd had any of his letters and stuff. I lied and said no. My father's come into some bucks. He said it was an income tax refund. But he never got a refund before. And he's been drinking so heavy. I think he's maybe in some trouble.''

I flashed the beam of my light through the doorway of the abandoned McCline Towing company offices and played it against the walls. ''Doing a little remodeling?''

''Burglars were here. Look at that far wall. I didn't touch that one yet.''

I had done it. ''What makes you think it's in Chinatown?''

''Todd had something his uncle wrote that made him think it was here. And then Todd killed himself. That's two people dead over this money, huh?''

''Maybe we can take you somewhere, Sonja? Someplace safe?''

''I'm okay. You're not going to let us look for the money?''

I shook my head.

After I helped her gather up a pry bar and a roofing hammer, I walked her up the stairs into the stairwell of the Milwaukee. Halfway up she halted, breathing heavily, and said, ''The funeral's tomorrow. I've never been to a funeral. I don't know how to act.''

''How about acting the way you feel?''

''I don't think I feel anything.''

''It gets like that.''

She flitted a delicate hand through her thick mop of dyed hair, letting sheaves flop in sequence. ''I keep having this nightmare that my father and Scotty Fogle had something to do with Todd's death.''

Later that night I watched the last hour of Lancaster, Marvin, and Strode in *The Professionals*. Before I turned in, I dialed the answer machine at the office.

Buzz ''Elroy'' Steeb.

''I hate talking on these machines. I don't know how to put this . . . I only wish . . . If you could come to my brother's services tomorrow. Really I'd like to go with you. My

parents . . . I don't want to be with them. It's at one tomorrow. Maybe you have to work or something? You don't have
to call me with an answer if you're too embarrassed to be
around a kid.''

He picked up the receiver on my first ring. "Buzz," I said,
"how about if I swing by around eleven-thirty?"

"You don't mind?"

"I'm glad you asked."

"Really?"

"My privilege."

23

IT WASN'T ANY KIND OF PRIVILEGE AT all. For starters, Bridget's relief for the day shift got drunk and didn't show, so Bridget was stuck doing twelve hours plus. After a few hasty phone calls I managed to hire Smithers to take up the slack. Smithers and I had joined the SPD at the same time. Affable, reasonably competent, he had a false and nearly insufferable sense of his own expertise accompanied by an inexplicable penchant for plump women, was fond of saying he was going to sharpen his harpoon and snag a date.

The morning of the funeral Judy called, sounding terse and a bit wrought. "Thomas? I've got some time this afternoon. Are you free by chance?"

She had *never* asked me out before.

"A week ago I would have been," I said reluctantly. "I've got an appointment I can't ditch. It could drag out."

"Oh."

"A funeral."

"I'm sorry to hear that. Anyone close?"

"Yes and no. I'll explain later. Make it this evening?"

When I went to the closet I found my one dark suit had wrinkled sleeves and a stain on the lapel. Kathy removed the stain, ironed the winkles, and was kind enough not to rag me about my inadequacies as a liberated male, normally a favored topic.

"Don't be so glum, Cisco." She pronounced it See-is-ko.

"I was just remembering when I quit my high school basketball team. It didn't crush the coach or anything, but I guess I had been identifying with Todd more than I knew."

"You two had a lot in common. Same with the younger one. He looks up to you."

"Does he?"

"Kids always like you."

From the turnout at Elmore Steeb's funeral one could easily imagine Franklin High School had been shut down. There were two days left in the official school calendar, and a lot of students must have been taking advantage of this sabbatical day. Todd hadn't been particularly important on campus, and at first I couldn't account for the remarkable turnout.

The services were held in the gargantuan Episcopal church on Capitol Hill near Volunteer Park. The place was floor to rafter with kids, most of whom were teary-eyed and probably wouldn't have known what Todd Steeb looked like if he'd croaked on their doorstep.

In the mistaken belief that numbers and a swanky exit furnished some sort of legitimacy to his son's life, Dudley Steeb had choreographed the fandango. The class president gave a speech. A school board member gave a speech. The principal spoke. A pretty cheerleader in uniform—everything but the pompons—stood at the podium and wept as she read a poem of her own that was surprisingly eloquent—and this to a background tape of Todd playing the piano. It was the first time I'd heard the dead boy's music. It was stunning.

Buzz and I and his parents and a coterie of Kleenex-clutching relatives sat in the front row. After the cheerleader gushed and right before the minister sermonized, Buzz coughed once and got up and walked directly down the aisle of that monstrous and magnificent Episcopalian church and out the tall doors into the drizzle of an overcast Monday afternoon. In doing so, he stalked past five hundred gaping people. I couldn't see his face. I could see only the curious and sympathetic looks on the young faces he passed.

Crossing his arms, he stood on the front steps alongside the thick marble pillars and watched the limousine drivers in their black livery. He remained tearless and slump-shouldered, looking as weary as a boy could look. When I reached him, I could hear the whistle of his breath through his nostrils.

"What a bunch of bullshit."

"Is that how you see it?" I said gently.

"That music. Now all of a sudden Dad thinks he was a great pianist. It was all grades and running when Todd was alive. Music was something Dad tolerated. Those kids are talking about Todd like he was one of them. He was never one of them."

"Most of them know that. They're doing their best to accord him some respect in the only way they know."

Buzz looked around at me. "You think so?"

"Sure."

"Everyone thinks he killed himself."

"I know."

"Todd wouldn't do that to me."

"Of course, he wouldn't, Buzz."

"He liked to run, and he liked to play, and he was just absolutely going to be the best or it was going to kill him. He never even tried very hard, and he was. He was *my* brother, goddammit. They're all in there talking like he was their brother."

"You're right. You two had something special. You can't manufacture another brother or the fourteen years of growing up with him. But other people feel bad also."

Buzz glanced around at the trees and the clumps of parked cars, hot rods, Japanese compacts, at the limousine awaiting the family and the hearse awaiting the deceased. For a minute, thinking about how much he'd lost and how most of it wasn't going to sink in until later, I came close to tears.

"You think Todd would mind if I skipped the rest of this?" he asked.

"I think Todd would be disappointed if you didn't."

Still determined not to cry, Buzz smiled a warped smile that knotted his cheeks up like chestnuts. "My parents wouldn't have said a thing like that in a jillion years."

"Your parents are hurting as much as you are."

"Think so?"

"Yes, I do."

Together, we shucked our ties and jackets and cruised the city in my Ford pickup. We meandered through the University of Washington campus, sometimes talking, sometimes mute, fed peanuts to the squirrels, reminisced about his brother, drifted through bookstores and boutiques and art galleries on University Way. I found out more that afternoon than I had in a week of investigating. Buzz had all of Jan Galloway's manuscript materials, hundreds of pages of notes and raw manuscripts. When we drove to his house and he gave them to me, I had to bite my tongue to keep from telling him I already had the money.

His parent's weren't home from the cemetery yet.

Buzz was obsessed with the money, figured if he could find it, he'd know how and why Todd died. I did my best to deflect that reasoning. I didn't want him hurt in a free-for-all scrabble for treasure.

We rode the elevator to the observation floor of the Columbia Center and stood next to the rainy windows and watched the scudding clouds and specks of the city that shone through.

"You have all those materials all the time?" I asked Buzz.

"No. Mom cleaned out all of Todd's things. Every last one. I got his watch and a couple of pairs of shoes. His state trophies. Everything else went to the Goodwill. She started at midnight two nights ago and worked until about three in the afternoon the next day. When the movers took his piano out of his room, all this stuff was inside. Luckily I was the only one home. It's all the stuff we found in Grandma's trunk. After her stroke she hardly kept any of her stuff. Just that trunk and a few other things. I remember what a big stink she made. Bury her, but don't bury the trunk. Mom thought she was senile."

"But Mom kept the trunk."

"Humoring her."

It was five o'clock when I finally dropped Buzz off in front of his house. He skipped nimbly up the front stairs and disappeared inside.

An hour later Judy Banner and I rendezvoused at the Poor Italian downtown near the old Moore Theater. We sat in the back. We ordered. She looked gorgeous, if a little tired. She was twitchy, kept adjusting her glasses with a pale hand that I wanted to fondle, but didn't. Something about her manner warned me off. Her car was on the street, parked a block from my truck. Neither of us had secured a hotel room. Without saying a word, we both knew something in our relationship had altered. I didn't know what, but I didn't like it.

"Busy weekend?" I asked.

"About normal. I got a little time off yesterday afternoon. I called your house, but you didn't answer."

"I was on a stakeout most of yesterday." That was twice she had called me.

"Fugitives from a chain gang? Rumrunners?" She smiled halfheartedly.

"A funny deal. I seem to be the only one in the world who thinks there's anything deeper than the cosmetics of the thing. So far we've caught two high school kids looking for buried treasure. I don't know. Maybe I'm wasting my time."

"Tell me about it."

I looked at her hazel eyes behind those reflecting glasses she wore like shields. "You've never wanted to hear about one of my cases, Judy. Why the sudden interest?"

She leaned both bare elbows on the table, set her chin in the cup formed by her folded hands, and gazed at me.

"Something's wrong, isn't it?" I said.

"Nothing."

"Sooner or later we have to talk."

"I want to know what you do for a living." Her voice was getting stronger, verging on strident but not angry yet.

"I'm a private detective. I told you that. I work mostly for an old friend, Kathy Birchfield. I find witnesses, verify alibis, look for lost kids. A prosecution witness is lying, I try to find out why and prove it, or discredit that person. It's mostly scrounging around in old records, interviewing ex-employers, and gossiping with snoopy neighbors. Right now I'm trying to tie up some loose ends on a teenage runaway who ended up dead. Suicide maybe."

"You must be good at what you do."

"Why do you say that?"

"Because you're confident you won't ever get caught."

"What does that mean?" The waitress served us while Judy sat on her reply. I had ordered ravioli; Judy, spinach salad.

"You promised when we started, you wouldn't spy on me."

"I haven't."

She began to cry, silently, without blinking. I'd never seen her cry before, and it was a revelation in a way that I cannot explain. There was something unnerving about it, as if I were somehow physically hurting her. Her hazel eyes looked like molten candy. "The only thing I ever wanted from you was a little time to get away from the rest of my life. I never wanted to get married or drag you away from other girl friends, this Kathy Birchfield—"

"Kathy's not a girl friend."

"Maybe you don't sleep together, but you should hear your voice when you talk about her."

"I haven't been spying."

She daubed at her face with a linen napkin and pushed her chair out. "I didn't want to tell you, and you promised you wouldn't pry. That was all we had, Thomas, that mutual trust."

"Judy," I pleaded softly.

Composing herself, she went to the rack, picked up her coat, slipped into it, and calmly walked out of the restaurant.

"Hell," I muttered, then ate my ravioli. I ate her salad. I left the biggest tip I'd left in years. When I finally exited the Poor Italian and strode out into the drizzle on Second Avenue, Judy's car was gone, and with it, whatever hope I'd had that this wouldn't be the bluest Monday in a long while.

24

KATHY AND I SAW EACH OTHER ONLY in snips and snatches all that week.

I finished reading *The Eunuch*, and despite my reservations about the author, I found myself once again enthralled by the world he'd created. Had *The Eunuch* played a part in Todd Steeb's quest? Rumors had abounded for years of a cult at the James house, and I wondered if Todd hadn't somehow gotten snared into something kinky.

When I rented the video, I saw now that Delores Del Rabo James was wildly miscast. Yet the film still worked as ingenious storytelling and titillation.

Besides keeping tabs on the Milwaukee and reading, I'd been pedaling my bicycle every day. Not far, twenty-five or thirty miles. Also, I'd been pumping iron and pounding a heavy bag in the back of the garage. Bridget and I were still alternating shifts, beginning to get chummy, spelling each other early with gifts of food and conversation. Smithers rotated with us occasionally. I was keeping careful records and running up a humongous bill. We planted three more microphones, two in the Milwaukee and one in the room where I'd found the money so that if anybody prowled, we'd know immediately. So far the stakeout was a bust.

Every time I telephoned Judy at work somebody told me

161

she wasn't there. When I phoned her at home, there was no reply.

After supper Saturday night I rattled around the house. Kathy was out carousing. The stakeout was being handled by stand-ins all weekend so Bridget could go hiking at Hurricane Ridge with her boyfriend and I could take a much needed break.

The previous day I had skipped my workout. I'd put myself through a light one that morning, and now I knew why.

I tugged on a pair of old jeans, shin and knee pads underneath, then steel-toed boots, which I laced up tightly and taped. I slipped a catcher's heavy athletic cup where it would do the most good. After skipping rope for fifteen minutes, I taped my knuckles until they felt as hard and knobby as hockey pucks, put on a heavy work shirt, a pair of leather driving gloves that had already been ruined, and ran into Kathy on the way out the back door. I almost knocked her down, had to catch her by the shoulders to keep her from falling backward.

Dressed for a night out, she halted on the steps and smiled up at me, her dark hair wild and thrown back as if she'd been riding a motorcycle.

"Thought you had a date," I said.

"A party. It was a bummer. Where are you going?"

"Stood up, eh?"

"Ah, don't look at me like that. He's a cop. I think he got stiffed with some overtime. And parties are no fun alone."

"Wanna have some fun?"

"Good-time Charlie. Where are you going dressed like a mechanic who lost his coveralls?"

"Not far. Saturday night with Thomas Black?"

"It's a scary thought, but I guess I have nothing better to do."

While I drove, Kathy filled me in on the details of a rape case she was defending, which, coincidentally, was the first case out of her new office I'd refused to work. It was fun to listen to her discourse. She read people well, knew their foibles, and her comments on various legal types in Seattle were always entertaining. When we arrived in the Mount

Baker neighborhood, I killed the motor and turned to her.
"What?" she said.

"You're a pistol. I like the way you get so enthusiastic."

"What's this place? McCline's? What are we doing here?"

I shrugged. Nobody answered when I rapped on the front
door. The rusted-out wheelbarrow was still in the yard. The
drapes were askew. I stumbled back to the truck and turned
the ignition, wondering if I should have called for an appoint
ment.

The J and M Tavern, a run-down bar on Rainier Avenue
between Walden and Genesee, produced immediate and
nerve-rattling results.

Chester McCline and Scotty Fogle were yukking it up with
a couple of blue-eyed fat women in jeans at a back table. The
stereo in the tavern was so loud you couldn't hear yourself
talk. From the look of things they'd just met the women.
Until I came in with Kathy, the four of them had been the
only white folk in the place. Now we were six, and all eyes
were on us. There must have been thirty-five other patrons.
At one end of the building a clot of players loitered around
the pool tables, the haze of tobacco smoke down almost
to their knees. It was a nice place. It looked like they washed
the tables once a week and the glasses when a big man com-
plained.

I strode all the way to the table before Chester or Scotty
noticed.

Picking up a loose cigarette, I dropped it into Chester
McCline's beer pitcher where it spun in a circle and sizzled
until it was dead. One of the chesty women squealed and
stood up, her chair tumbling onto its spine.

"Well, well," said McCline over the music, "the private
dick rented hisself a nut sack."

"And he come here to become extinct," said Scotty Fogle.

Fogle wore a cowboy hat, a large turquoise buckle on his
belt, and a grin that made his long teeth look like fork tines.
McCline wore penny loafers, slacks, and an exquisitely
pressed Hawaiian shirt. I wondered who did his laundry.
Probably Sonja.

"Where do you want to do this?" I asked.

"Out back?" McCline was staring daggers in an effort to intimidate me.

"Make sure nobody interferes." I glanced around the room at the dark faces. A couple of big men sat at the bar. Nobody else in the saloon except the woman bartender was big enough or young enough to hurt me. At least not one at a time.

McCline said, "I don't need no help with pansies."

"Only high school kids?"

McCline leaned his nearly hairless forearms on the table and gave me a look that was a virtual death threat. Then his eye got caught by the rose I'd stuck into a buttonhole on my shirt. He leaned back and twisted his face in disbelief, then snickered. "Five minutes?"

"I'm ready now."

"Gotta relieve myself."

Outside at the truck Kathy grabbed one of my shoulders. "Are you crazy, Thomas? Get in that truck right now and make tracks. I'm going to call the police. Get in that truck. Move it."

"And break a date?"

"Yeah? Why you?"

"See anybody else volunteer?"

"That's good, Thomas. That's real clever. He's an animal. His arms are as big around as your legs."

"Most of that's fat."

"What about the part that's not? Are you nuts? What's this?"

I handed her my .45 automatic. "They get me down and start putting the boots to me, shoot 'em."

"Wait a minute . . ."

"Okay, put a round into the ground. You know how to use that thing. I just don't want to get my brains stomped flat while everybody's standing around with their thumbs up their asses. There's a clip in it. Ram a cartridge into the chamber and you're ready for business. You know how to use it."

Breathing deeply, I handed Kathy my wallet and headed around the tavern. She shouted after me, "One of those creeps gets you down I'll blow his friggin' brains out." She jammed the gun into her handbag and spoke breathlessly. "What do you mean, *they*? You're not going to take on *both*?"

"Don't see any choice."

"Thomas?"

A small crowd of interested patrons had assembled. Betting had begun. Kathy refused some pretty decent odds before she put ten bucks down: me over McCline. In an alley fight you'd be surprised how wimpy a rose in your lapel can make you look. Winking at me, she put down another five that said the tall guy in the cowboy hat wouldn't stay out of it.

When McCline and Fogle strutted through the group, overconfident grins slit their faces. I was six-one and 180, but I didn't look that heavy. Nor did I look particularly street-wise. As usual I was counting on my opponents to underestimate me. Fogle was taller than I remembered and moved more solidly. McCline was wider and heavier than I remembered. They both were older than I was.

Who knew how long they'd been drinking? No doubt they were numb to pain. I could see by Kathy's nervous eyes she thought I had about as much chance as a raw egg on a school bus.

McCline was sounding out the ground rules when I slammed Fogle in the throat with the side of my hand. Gasping for breath, he hunched over, eyeballs ready to burst. I hit him as hard as I could in the ribs. He spun in a circle and, gasping and writhing, draped his torso around a heavy man's ankles.

McCline's face turned beet red, and he took two unsteady steps forward, fists on his hips. "This was between you and me, asshole."

"Now it is."

I tagged his nose and watched him stagger backward six paces. It was my last freebie.

25

WHEN HE REACHED UP AUTOMATI-
cally with both hands to pat his face, his left hand had a club
in it. Smaller than a cricket bat, scarred from use and three
feet in length, it resembled something the Indians might have
used to slaughter porpoises.

Face lightly smeared with blood, McCline waded into me,
swinging heavily muscled arms, the bat whirring in the air
like a propeller.

The tide of onlookers didn't split apart fast enough for
either of us, and as I backed up, I trampled a skinny man
while McCline slugged some whining guy in the arm on a
backswing. McCline missed three times in a row, fanning
the air between us, a low, deadly vibration emanating from
the wooden bat. He didn't care if he missed. He had me
retreating. He was swinging at my teeth.

I tried to dance, but the crowd didn't give me enough
room. He caught me with a whack to the gut.

Despite the sudden racking pain, I tangled the bat up by
flipping my arm down on it and clamping it tightly against
my rib cage.

Stepping close as he tried to wrest the war club away, I
threw him over my hip. He resisted, had had some judo, but
I threw him anyway. Until now he had underestimated me
as badly as any man could. I tried to crunch his fingers with

my boot as he was getting up, but in the jostling and hooting, amid the beer-guzzling spectators, I missed my fat little targets.

To make up for it, I booted him in the face.

They booed me hardily. I was getting no points for style. McCline got up anyway. And he still had the bat, still had the grin, bloodier now, took one swing on the way up, and thumped one of my shin protectors. Foresight had saved me a broken leg. His shirt wasn't even rumpled.

It was going to be a long night.

I lost track of where Kathy was. And Scotty Fogle, too, though somebody seemed to have dragged him away and hustled him out of the makeshift gravel arena we'd forged between the parked Buicks and Hondas.

While we fought, a spring rain began to fall, spotty and heavier than it should have been, the type that soaked you before you realized it.

McCline swung once, twice, and I ducked and jumped back and stumbled over something, falling heavily. Later on I figured that was where I sprained my wrist. Kathy told me it was Scotty Fogle's lanky legs that I'd sprawled over, Fogle having deliberately rolled into the fray to trip me.

Before I could regain my feet, McCline was over me with the bat, gave me one good whack to the middle of my forehead with the butt end of it. As he was doing it, you could see he was holding back. The expert. Just enough juice to knock me cold. He didn't need a murder conviction.

A jolt of lightning twanged my neck, and I flipped and rolled and lay still on my face. The spectators mumbled. The raindrops slapped one side of my face gently, the opposite side chewed by sharp gravel.

McCline stepped toward me. I could hear the gravel under his heavy tread.

I thought I could rush him with my forearms covering my head and he'd get another whack in and then we'd be man to man, but I didn't think I could do it before Kathy shot him.

Amid the catcalls and jeering and hoots, I heard the muffled sound of her jacking a round into the chamber of the automatic—still in her large handbag. She could easily be misjudging my toughness against McCline's quickness and land herself in a heap of trouble. I couldn't yell to her not to shoot because then everybody would know she had a gun and somebody was likely to grab it. That was all we needed.

Though I was certain I could get my legs under me and spring into McCline, knock him down, I was just as certain it wouldn't look that way to her. When I'd caught her eye a few moments ago, she'd been nervous as a ferret in a box.

I played possum, hoping McCline wouldn't take another swing. Hoping Kathy wouldn't fire a cap. Into the ground or into McCline. He kept out of range.

"You done got him," somebody said.

"My, my," said a woman with a southern drawl. "That lasted a mite longer than I thought it would. He be a tough nut."

"Shore warn't no boxer," said McCline.

Nobody much cared if I had been rendered dead or just permanently stupid. By the time Kathy knelt beside me, they were on their way inside, gravel crunching, money changing hands, laughter marking their passage. "Thomas?"

"Natasha?"

"You weren't . . ."

"I thought you were going to shoot him."

"You bet I was going to shoot him, Boris. He was about to beat your head like a paddle ball."

"Too much exercise for a fatty like him."

Standing up slowly, I brushed myself off and let the rain pelt my hot face. I was only a little dizzy. Head shots are funny. Some of them wipe you out for a month or forever, and others bounce right off. During the fight I'd been thinking about Todd Steeb's encounter with McCline and Fogle, Todd's begging, calling them sir, and the more I thought about it, the angrier I got.

Smiling drunkenly from a semireclining position on the ground, Scotty fixed me with a daffy look and clutched at his ribs. I swung hard and put the toe of one of my boots into his shoulder. He rolled, screamed, moaned. One of the fat women who had stayed to nurse him cursed me.

Thinking I was going to do more damage, Kathy pulled me away. "Thomas, he was already down."

"Now he'll be down longer."

Inside the tavern I located the other white woman right away, but McCline was nowhere to be seen. The rumble of music had resumed, and the curtain of smoke had sunk down to waist level. I watched the woman's eyes swing toward the men's rest room in the back. Nobody made a move to stop me. They all thought I was fuddled from the blow, that I was about to get annihilated. A few grinned in anticipation. One friendly man shook his head and gave a warning scowl.

The rest rooms were at the end of a stubby cramped corridor. The door was unlocked.

I saw the stick standing against the washbasin beside McCline and kicked it away before he realized who I was. Then I kicked him in the thigh. He crashed backward against the wall, knotting his hammy hands into fists as the wall sounded off from the impact. He had been washing blood off his face.

He reached for the stick, which had slid across the floor and smacked into the wall nearby, but I stepped inside and caught him with an uppercut. Then another.

Rolling backward, he half fell against the sink, then brought a fist forward almost from the floor, aimed at my family jewels. I blocked his blow, but the power in his swing hurt my crossed forearms. The room was cramped. My blows to his head had done very little damage. Head shots weren't going to be the ticket with this guy. I stepped back and snapped off a kick at his knees, once, twice, connecting hard. The pain threw him forward so that he vaulted onto me.

Face buried in my side, he lunged, carrying me across the tiny room and we did an odd waltz. We boomed into a metal garbage can, the wall, the commode stall, ripping bolts out of the floor, and the washbasin, tearing it off the wall. Water squirted across my legs and flushed the floor. We began sliding. He had me in a bear hug, smashing at my chin with his head, butting, and then we skidded, spun, and together our heads shattered the cheap mirror on the wall on our way down.

For a long while we wrestled in the water, punching at each other's faces when we got elbowroom. I could feel him progressively getting weaker. I only had to keep him from gouging out an eyeball or ripping off a stray ear. And then we were on our feet again and bashing like a couple of testy linemen trying out for a pro football team. It was only when I danced him around and jammed his ass hard into the broken pipes from the sink twice that he loosened his grip around my torso enough for me to slam a palm upward into his chin.

Now I was loose.

I tattooed his head and neck with blows.

Half blind in his own blood, he roared and swung wildly twice, connecting against my arms and shoulders. I'd cut him. His eye sockets were puddles of thick, scummy blood.

Working my arms like pistons, I moved to the body and pounded. He went down once. I let him straggle up, and we went at it again. I tried to pound him in nonvital spots, targeting ribs and muscle rather than organs that would bleed internally. I didn't want to kill him, just make him feel as if I had.

"Okay. Okay," he muttered finally, and oozed to the floor on his rump.

His pants were half torn off. One leg was completely out, and he'd lost that shoe, his foot dragging around a sopping wet argyle sock that had stretched out like a tongue.

He lay wedged into the corner next to the broken sink, gasping and bleeding profusely from the cuts on his brow, from his nostrils, and from a laceration on the side of his scalp. The whole room was a Jackson Pollock of blood, water, broken glass, and bits of dusty wallboard. It would be awhile before he sailed into a fight as handsomely as he'd sailed into this one. We'd made a god-awful racket, and I could hear the curious crowd milling outside. I kicked at the slowly opening bathroom door, causing it to slam shut with a sound like a gunshot.

"Time for show and tell," I said. "Why did you beat on Todd Steeb?"

"Fuck you," he said, with a wet lisp, blood spattering out with his words.

I put the toe of my boot to his bare thigh and nudged.

"You fucker," he spit.

I kicked him solidly. Then I half picked him up and rammed him facefirst into the door. Spinning him around, I grabbed him by the collar until we both heard fabric shredding. The brawl had drained him of resistance. Half blind, bleeding, ribs cracked, he was only waiting to see how badly I would main him.

Holding his hands in front of his face to signal "no more," McCline caught his breath and said, "The kid had some jewelry. I saw his uncle with some of it before he quit me. Years ago. Back in the early sixties." He hacked and spit a gob of blood across the room. It stuck low on the wall.

"Jan Galloway?"

"Right. Yeah. That's the fucker."

"What jewelry?"

"Old rings and necklaces and stuff. Worth a bundle."

"What else did you see Galloway with twenty-eight years ago?"

"Hell, we were still working out of Chinatown. I kept him on more out of charity than anything. He was always beefing about raises and shit. What else? I dunno. He quit me. You done, or what?"

"Where did he get the jewelry?"

McCline hunkered over and tried to catch his breath. I'd suffered broken ribs in the past. He wasn't going to breathe easily for several months.

"Wish I knew. I never really figured it out until years later. He had these rings, a couple of them, said they were his grandmother's. Bullshit. Stole 'em somewheres. Then he upped and quit. I shoulda looked into it, but I didn't think of it until his nephew gave Sonie that ring. Looked just like one a the others."

"You're lying, McCline. You've been in this thing all along."

"I don't know what you're talking about." He slowly sat on the floor, surrounded by dirty water, toilet cakes, and soggy cigarette butts. The fleshy lower half of his stomach showed under his tattered Hawaiian shirt. You could almost feel sorry for the guy.

"Did something happen in the International District twenty-eight years ago?" I asked, stabbing for the truth.

"Nothin'."

"You know there's cash laying around, don't you? Even today. Todd Steeb had thirty grand his father found under his bed."

"Shit. A kid like that with thirty grand, he'd piss it away."

"Not like you. You could spend it on loose women and bad booze and slow horses, and then you could give the rest to charity, eh?"

"I don't know what you're talking about. Galloway got himself some goods, that's all I know. Stole 'em. Hadda. Maybe he was a cat burglar. Maybe he was peddlin' stolen cars."

McCline fanned his hands up in front of his face, thinking I was going to pummel him again.

"You killed Todd, didn't you?"

"Me?"

"Better talk. I don't know what I'm liable to do."

"They're calling the cops out there," he said, rolling his blood-rimmed blue eyes wildly toward the door.

"Not likely. They think you won. They're not going to call the cops."

"He said it himself. 'I'm too sorry.' He killed himself. What's with you? Does a guy have to rent a billboard before you believe him?"

I pulled the door open against the ponderous weight of his legs, squeezed through the crowd of curious faces outside, and grabbed Kathy's arm. As I towed her away, she scooped money out of several hands.

"There's some shit on the floor of your bathroom," I said to nobody in particular.

She turned to me, and I could feel the wind from her words on my cheek. "I thought he was killing you."

"He got his licks in."

"You were absolutely brutal."

"Thanks."

"It wasn't a compliment."

"Maybe I should go back and apologize."

"To those bastards?" She snatched the tattered rose I'd put back in my lapel and sniffed it, her lips curling into a Madonna smile. "Thomas?"

"Huh?"

"You really know how to show a girl a good time."

Sunday mornings had been a ritual with Kathy Birchfield and me—back when she was in law school and I was a cop. She would come upstairs in a robe and jammies, I'd be in jeans and a T-shirt, and together we'd whip up a batch of biscuits and pop them into the oven. One of us would stir up a couple of quarts of orange juice or apple cider, and we'd sit down over the morning paper and exchange war stories about our week, all the while smothering biscuits in margarine and honey.

If the day was perfect, the sun would jet down through the trees in my backyard and warm up the kitchen and put a little sparkle into her blue-violet eyes and a little shine on the shin she tucked up under her hips.

"How are you feeling?" she asked.

"A few kinks. The tooth fairy was by and loosened some of my favorites. They'll tighten."

"How's your head? I thought he killed you when he hit you with that stick."

"Just a bruise."

"Must have hit you in the brain."

"Ha-ha."

After a while Kathy said, "I haven't heard much about Judy lately. You two still on?"

"Depends on how you define 'on.' "

"I'm sorry to hear that. Want to talk?"

"Later."

But she wasn't sorry. She could hardly keep from laughing aloud.

She said, "I've been reading *The Autobiography of Delores Del Rabo*. You see it?"

"I skimmed it."

"What an egomaniac."

"Comes with the territory."

"Not like her. She had two kids out of wedlock when she was in her early twenties and actually gave them away so she could concentrate on her career. She claims she was Marilyn Monroe's best friend for a number of years and that Marilyn secretly kept her from stardom. Claims J. Edgar Hoover secretly kept her from stardom. Eisenhower was supposedly writing letters to studio execs in Hollywood trying to sink her career." Kathy tilted her chair back on two legs. "This whole thing has hit you pretty hard, hasn't it?"

"Me?"

"You're on the skids with a woman you'd cut your right arm off for, and you hardly mention it."

"I want to know who killed Todd."

"You're sure he was killed? Nobody else is."

"He was."

Kathy pulled four hundred dollars out of the pocket in her thin paisley robe and slapped it onto the table.

"What's this?"

"I bet fifty on Fogle getting involved and a hundred and fifty on you to box McCline to the ground before the police got there."

"Where's your share?" I said, scooping up the bills.

"It was your money. I got it out of your wallet."

"You what?"

26

SUNDAY AFTERNOONS ARE A BONAN-
za for convalescent homes. Everybody trots off to church and
gets slammed in the conscience, and right after the sermon
but before mall shopping they tote along flowers and phony
smiles and tell granny how great she's looking.

Clutching a fistful of roses and flashing a rubbery smile,
I signed in at Pleasant Vista among the old gummers pushing
walkers and their visiting sons and daughters.

"Thomas." I turned around, startled.

Buzz Steeb had shaved the sides of his head, sculpted the
remainder of his hair into a Mohawk, dyed the fuzz on top
orange, and tipped it in Lincoln green. If you went for that
sort of spectacle, it wasn't done poorly. He'd probably
skinned his skull with a razor I bought him. He wore a ripped
football jersey, running shorts, and a pair of New Balance
cross-country shoes. Tattoos speckled one bare arm; real or
paste-ons, I could not tell. He was diffusing the hurt with
silliness. Amid the tiny hearts and skulls were "Born to
Lose," "Who Cares?," and "Fuck em!"

"Buzz, my boy." I grinned and shook his limp hand.
"Here to see Leona?"

"She's not much today. Didn't recognize us." He jiggled
a leg nervously. He looked a wreck. Farther up the green-
walled corridor Faith and Dudley Steeb emerged from Leona

175

Galloway's room, waving good-bye to the old lady and speaking with a hollow-sounding gaiety.

"What have you been up to?" I asked.

"Not much," said Buzz.

"Me neither. Still running?"

"Six miles this morning." He rubbed his nose on the palm of his hand. "It's not the same."

"It wouldn't be. By the way, have you talked to anybody about what was in Todd's note?"

Buzz looked as if he was going to flee. "I haven't talked to anybody about anything."

He moved off when his parents approached, as if the four of us in proximity might create some sort of cataclysmic implosion. I shouted after him, "Give me a call sometime. I'm still working on the case."

"Yeah. Sure."

He stumbled off, bowlegged, in that deerlike way of moving that he had, gawky and quick.

Faith Steeb barely glanced at me, stumbled past, muttering a quick hello and a quicker good-bye. Dudley, in his Sunday best, keys jangling somewhere under his coat like bells on a reindeer, stopped in front of me and squared himself up with my shoulders. Contorting his face in exaggerated motions, he inched his lips down over his teeth several times and stared hard into my eyes.

"We smell money, don't we? Always a little man sniffing around the smell of the green stuff, isn't there?"

"Don't give me any bull. I'm not working for you anymore, so I don't have to be polite."

"Were you ever?"

"Nobody's scrounging. I'm here because your oldest son is dead and it wasn't suicide. I'm working on my own time with my own money, and when this gets cleared up, if it gets cleared up, maybe I'll tell you about it."

Steeb's face paled. His steady eyes turned watery. "What are you really working on, Black?"

"I told you."

"You're investigating America's Carpets, aren't you?"

"Is your conscience that guilty?"

"What have you uncovered?"

"That's not how it works. You hire me, I talk. Otherwise, you'll just have to read about it in the funny papers."

"Okay. You're hired."

"Forget it. I like it this way."

Casting a forlorn look down the dim green hallway, Steeb worked his lower jaw as if he had something in his mouth he had to get rid of. His voice was beginning to quiver in the long vowels. "You don't have to talk to her. She doesn't have anything."

"I am sorry about your boy. I liked him a lot."

Dudley raised both hands and clapped them to his face. He wept silently. It was so abrupt I might have thought he was joking if I hadn't known better. "If I'd realized he was going to leave us . . . I said so many angry things I need to take back. Now Buzz has started to go off the deep end. I don't know how to manage him. In the end I'll have lost them both. God!"

A uniformed nurse's aide bustled past, ignoring Dudley's outburst.

"Wish I could help you, Mr. Steeb."

"Nothing means anything. Not the business. Not the investments. All wasted. All that time with him is gone. I killed the boy."

"Give me that again?"

"I killed him," he said. The confession froze our conversation, and then Dudley, realizing what he'd admitted, looked into my eyes. "Not like you think. I wanted to control him. Wanted him to be part of my carpet empire. I was so damn inflexible. They say he was a genius on that piano, and I wanted him to sell carpets. It was my inattention that killed him."

"Nonsense."

"What?"

"You might have been a better father, but you didn't kill him. Either he killed himself, and if he did that, he was big enough to know what was happening, or somebody else knocked him off, in which case you don't have an exclusive contract on guilt."

"The father of a dead son can't escape guilt."

"You may be right about that."

"Faith even blames me."

"What do you remember about your brother-in-law's money?"

"Nothing."

"You knew Todd found bundles of cash?"

He gave me a sharp, weepy look. "Yes."

"And you knew who it belonged to."

My suggestion ignited the light behind his pale blue eyes. "Even though Todd denied it, I guess I knew all along it was Jan's money. Black, we're trying to forget, not rake up our mistakes. I shouldn't even be talking to you." He stumped down the corridor toward the front door, mopping at his face with a clean handkerchief.

"Dudley," I said, "have you told anybody about the note?"

Without turning, he shook his head and continued walking away.

Leona was alone. Under a shabby shawl she sat hunched in the same chair. She might not have budged an inch in the week since I'd seen her last.

"Mrs. Galloway?"

Slowly she focused, knitting her thick brows together, the hairs on her face inching around like caterpillar whiskers. "I met you," she finally said.

"Maybe a week ago. With your grandson Buzz."

"Buzz was just here. I didn't talk to him."

"I saw him in the hallway."

"Buzz was just here." She scrutinized my face. "The jaybirds whistled, and the vultures danced."

"Ma'am?"

It took her a long time to reply, but when she did, she was lucid. "It's an old song. Haven't been able to get it out of my noggin. A railroad song. My first husband was a gandy dancer. Horrible hard work on the railroad. What do you want?"

"I brought some flowers."

"I can *see*. What do you want?"

I set the flowers on her dresser and then sat myself on the bed opposite her chair. "Mrs. Galloway, I need to know anything you can tell me about your son, Jan, and the money he came across in December of 1959."

"He was going to give it back."

"And?"

"Vowed to give it back. Every red cent. It ate at his poor heart for years. He didn't like to know he was a thief. Except something happened."

"What?"

"Can't rightly recollect."

"Your stroke?"

"Fiddledeedee." Her voice rose. "I lost everything. Half my damn life is gone like bath water. Surely wish I could get it back."

"Your stroke was after your son's death, wasn't it?"

"A couple of weeks."

"You wrote a letter to a man named Carstens. Recall that?"

"No."

"You remember a lot today," I said.

A female voice came from behind. "She does that. Comes in and out." A tiny Asian woman, about half my weight, lugged a sack of soiled bedding across the room. She commenced busily removing the bedclothes on the far bed. I started to get up, but she waved me off. "No, no. Keep talking. Just be a minute."

"Was Dudley involved with the money?" I asked.

"He started the rug business with Jan."

"Did he have anything to do with the money?"

"Couldn't honestly tell you. Wish I had my life back. Lived all those years, and now I can't recall them. Isn't that a pickle to be in? Some days I don't know my own rear end from a can of buttermilk."

"We all get those days."

"I remember when I was a child, the fishman and the vegetable peddlers came around once a week in their horse-drawn wagons. We used to take the smaller spuds and save them so we could use them on the spouts of the kerosene cans. The iceman came around, and we children used to suck on chips of ice.''

Then she looked at the wall and changed channels, and except for the woman working on the far bed, I was alone.

The Asian woman glanced up from her work, smiled at me, and said, ''She get like that. Her head funny.''

''How long until she comes back?''

''Hard to say. Sometime one day. Sometime only hours. She very tired.''

''There a doctor on duty?''

''Dr. Vogel.''

Before I left I pressed a picture of a young boy sitting on a seawall into the old lady's hands.

In her early thirties, Dr. Vogel was a gracious woman with a hawk nose, wan skin, and milk chocolate eyes that were too pretty for the rest of her. Out of shape, she had lumpy hips and a lax grip. She dressed smartly and talked in clipped, businesslike tones. I liked her. I inquired about Leona Galloway's memory.

It might be weeks, years, or never, explained Dr. Vogel. The only way we would ever know how much of her memory would return would be to sit back and wait. After her cerebral vascular accident Leona Galloway had been bedridden for three months. Her recovery was sporadic at best.

Almost as an afterthought I asked the doctor if I might see a roster of patients for the facility. After I read it, she said, ''Something wrong?''

I pointed out a name. ''What room?''

''One-oh-three in the basement. We keep those patients segregated because the basement exits directly onto the sidewalk. It's easier if we ever have to evacuate.''

''Keeps them out of sight, too.''

She hesitated. ''That might be part of it. I'd better come with you.''

The basement smelled of stinky socks and urine. Each of the eight rooms housed a tragedy: corpselike oldsters lying in bed like something out of Dachau, a grossly deformed and apparently mentally deficient woman in a wheelchair, and, in the room I'd come to view, a man in a specially built chair, strapped in, facing the window, motionless. There was little to look at outside the window except shrubs and a concrete wall.

Walking to the man in 103, I knelt, touched one of his deformed hands, and said, "Jim?"

He didn't reply.

"He can't hear very well," said Dr. Vogel. "Nor can he answer." She named the disease and gave the specifics of its progression, specifics I wasn't interested in.

"How long has he been here?"

"Two years, going on three."

"Family?"

"Wife. It hit her real hard. She had a collapse. She talks to him in a sort of code. He taps his hand. Takes them forever. She used to virtually live here. In fact, she took care of him at home for a while before her breakdown. He's told her never to see him again. That he's at peace."

"How long?"

"He'll probably last another year. Maybe nine months. He's had no remissions, just a steady deterioration. Don't worry. He wants us all to be very candid."

On the bedstead next to the tall hospital surplus bed stood a wedding photo of the man with his bride. He had been tall and athletic, though not particularly handsome. Now he was an amorphous lump, facial features contorted and unrecognizable.

The doctor overlaid my thoughts with something I didn't need to hear. "She comes several times a week, and he always tells her to go away. It hurts him to think her life is dribbling away while she waits for him to die. But she'll never stop visiting." Vogel said that last for the patient. The case had become personal.

A vague soughing sound came out of the man's throat, but neither the doctor nor I could decipher it. I patted him on his rounded shoulder and said, "Nice meeting you, Jim." I was lying. There hadn't been anything nice about it.

27

THE SEATTLE CENTER WAS FULL OF MU-
sic, squealing children, and carnival games. All of it con-
spired to turn me morose.

At the kiosk in the Science Center I bought a ticket to the
laser show, trooped in with the others, and lay back in the
dark to watch the colored lights zip and fizz on the domed
ceiling to the rhythm of synthesizer music. I kept thinking
how much Jim might like the show.

Afterward I took an amble through the sunshine and
crowds, found my truck on Thomas Street, and drove to West
Seattle.

Delores James wore a dress cut low in front. In the harsh
afternoon light I could see where her face had been tucked,
stitched, and zippered. Around her neck, she wore the coiled
boa constrictor, greens and browns, his bullet head and dart-
ing tongue dangling below her tiny waist like some sort of
Freudian atrocity.

"Delores," I said, "just read your autobiography. Extraordinary document. Never read anything quite like it."

It took her ten seconds to figure my angle as starstruck.
"Thank you, dear."

"Clayton home?"

"Gallivanting around on that damned wheel of his. Why?"

"He been out to Carstens's place near Fall City?"

Striking a pose out of one of her old flicks, she narrowed her eyes, one tweezed brow arching into a critical and slightly mischievous zigzag. "Carstens has passed on, don't you know?"

"How about yourself? You been out there? Ever talk to Clayton about it?"

Peering through the landscaped front yard to the street, past the faded azaleas, the full-blown peonies, the newly budded climbing roses, she ascertained that I was alone, then let out a small, satisfied purr. "I don't get out much. Why do you ask?"

"Just tying up some loose ends on this Steeb business."

"He was by again. Young Steeb's father. He came with a man who looked like a marine drill sergeant we'd had as an adviser on *This War Is for Gods*."

"His name McCline?"

"I believe that's what he called himself."

"What did they want?"

"Steeb accused Clayton of influencing his boy to commit suicide. The gall. I told him Clayton is the gentlest man I've ever known. Then they wanted to know if we gave the boy money."

"What happened?"

"Clayton got stern and tossed them out."

"About the funding for *The Eunuch*?"

"You'll have to wait for Clay. All this talk of money." She waved a hand in front of her face to fan herself and the snake.

At a pay phone at Thirty-fifth and Barton I phoned Sonja McCline. A blast of rock music boomed out of the receiver behind her mousy voice.

"Sonja?"

"This is."

"Thomas Black. I see you're still at home. How've you been?"

"I guess I'm all right. Moving in two days."

"Good for you."

"I've been thinking about it. The way you found me and

Bobby Hendrickson in Chinatown. You're investigating Todd's death, aren't you?''

"He was too smart for suicide, Sonja. Where does your father run his tow truck business?''

"On Aurora near Haller Lake. Some old lady who doesn't know what her property is worth rents him a lot cheap for car storage.''

"Will he be around today?''

"He got into a car wreck last night with Scotty. They went fishing in Scotty's boat. Up near Sekiu.'' Three, almost four hours away, Sekiu was a fishing village on the Strait of Juan de Fuca. Sportsmen berthed boats there so they'd have quick access to the salmon runs.

"Listen, Sonja, I want your help. Do you know where your father keeps his old records?''

"In the attic at his office. We keep our Christmas stuff there, too. And Mom's old clothes.''

"Can you get me in?''

"Sure. I'm not scared of him. What's he going to do?''

MCCLINE'S TOWING was just another invisible sign over an obscure building among the shops, storefronts, service stations, and video stores that clung to Aurora Avenue like barnacles. We swung into a wide gravel drive and approached a paint-chipped aluminum-walled building. In back were the tow trucks, five small ones and a beefier version. To the side was the holding yard, filled with recent wrecks, older hulks, and junk. Two ratty-looking guard dogs yapped at us from inside the cyclone fence.

"Dad's a slob,'' said Sonja, opening the front door.

A barnlike aqua structure with a gambrel roof, McCline's office consisted of a short, scarred counter, a file cabinet, three desks, a couple of beat-up couches, a TV, and a pop machine. Girly calendars. A small room in the back had a commode and changing bench. Deflated monkey suits dangled on hooks. At the rear of the building Sonja showed me a makeshift second-story loft. A rickety wooden ladder was the only way up.

When I climbed the steep rungs behind Sonja, my shoulders ached from the drubbing her father had given me. While the girl watched. I pawed through the dusty cardboard filing boxes. She rested on one leg, hands twined behind her rump, observing me carefully, as she had since the moment I picked her up. Her breath was humid with booze.

Slob or not, McCline had neatly filed his records by year and month. I pried the lid off the box labeled "1959" and squatted in the dust with it. "Whatcha looking for?" Sonja asked.

"I'm not sure," I lied.

The boxes were jammed with receipts, copies of towing bills, and hundreds of white forms, all wrinkled and grease-stained. They delineated the make, license number, owner, and driver of every call pulled by McCline's Towing that year. The only driver's names I recognized were McCline, Scotty Fogle, whose real first name was Harold, and Jan Galloway. I began making stacks, isolating the jobs Jan Galloway had driven. I checked all the December dates. I thought I was going to have to sort for hours, but it jumped out at me. Only it wasn't a Galloway job.

A Sunday evening. A 1951 Rolls-Royce. I had the owner and the driver, who were not the same, and the accident, which had occurred at the intersection of Empire Way and Cherry. The driver had been sent to Maynard Hospital, which no longer existed. The car had been towed to McCline's old lot on Jackson Street.

The report didn't state whether or not there had been passengers in the vehicle, only that Chester McCline had been driving the wrecker and that he'd hauled the Rolls to his yard on Jackson Street. Two days later the car was reclaimed by Beacon Hill Foreign Repair Specialists.

And that was that.

Except the same Sunday night Jan Galloway had rushed to his mother's house and slapped enough cash into her hands to pay off her mortgage. According to the records, Galloway had stopped driving for McCline a week later. The next year Galloway and Dudley Steeb founded America's Carpets. Success. Until six years ago, when Galloway jumped from a roof.

Pawing through stacks of towing records, I found three

others signed by Chester McCline. I compared the signatures. Now, with these old towing receipts in my hand, I thought I had the key to the jigsaw. The funny thing was, I was no closer to jailing a culprit.

Sonja hunkered in the dust beside me and did something bold for a girl just out of high school: She grasped my hand and examined the bruised knuckles, holding them so close to her face I could feel her breath on them. I'd taped and gloved them last night, but they'd taken a beating anyway. She touched a nick on my cheek.

She said, "They didn't have a car accident. I thought it was goofy 'cause there was nothing wrong with the car. It was you?"

I nodded. Our eyes locked.

"Let's get out of here," I said, quickly packing the boxes away.

On the way to the truck she said, "I shouldn't have brought you here."

"You told me your dad had come into some money?"

"He's buying a new car. He's never done that before." Tears flooded her dark eyes. "My father killed Todd, didn't he? Him and Scotty. And now I'm helping send him to jail, huh?"

For a variety of reasons I was afraid to answer that.

She said, "I called at work and asked George—Dad's garage foreman—if Dad and Scotty were around the day Todd died. They left real early. I think they tried to get Todd to tell them where the money was, and when he wouldn't . . ."

I had spoken to George last week and learned the same thing, had been led to the same suspicion. "Wait a week or two before you say anything about this, okay? Some of the dust should have settled."

"I hate him," she said. "And I hate you for getting him."

28

JUDY BANNER'S APARTMENT WAS A stucco building on the east slope of Queen Anne Hill and sported a partial view of Lake Union along with a full view of Capitol Hill and the sliding ribbon of lights on the freeway beneath the greenbelt. Sunday night. Traffic was sparse. The city sulked under a canopy of warm summer air. A skein of high, thin clouds scudded in from the south.

She came home a little after nine in the thickening dusk.

Five minutes later I knocked at her door.

"Thomas?" Gathering her composure, she said, "I was visiting relatives on Whidbey Island. I didn't expect to see you . . . again."

"I drove up to Pleasant Vista today."

As she unfolded a hand to position her glasses properly, her face tightened and the white skin around her eyes crinkled. I adored the way she did that, touching the hinge of her glasses authoritatively with one pale finger. Her brown hair was frizzing at the temples, from a windswept ferry ride no doubt. The sun had taken its toll, for her nose and cheeks were pink.

"I don't know that we really have anything to talk about, Thomas."

"Today at Pleasant Vista I visited a woman named Leona Galloway."

187

"I know what you were doing at Pleasant Vista," she said, trying to close the door.

"Galloway's the grandmother of a boy I was hired to find. A runaway. When I finally caught up with him about a week ago, he was on his face behind a three-story fall. The police and his folks think it was suicide." The door inched open. Her hazel eyes were curious. "It's been a bad couple of weeks. I lost the boy. Then I lost you. I decided to talk to the doctor about this Galloway lady. The doc gave me a roster of patients for Pleasant Vista."

Judy tucked her upper lip under her teeth, chewed it, inhaled deeply enough to make her nostrils flare and watched me. "Come in."

Her words were stark and didn't hint that any sympathy was going to blossom. She closed the door so softly I didn't hear it latch, politely offered me coffee, which I declined, then sat on the sofa.

It was a comfortable one-bedroom apartment. I'd been there before, although never more than a few minutes at a pop, to pick her up or drop her off. It contained no family pictures, memorabilia, almost nothing of a personal nature.

"You weren't spying on me?" she asked.

"You saw my name on the sign-in sheet, and you figured I could be there for only one reason. I would have thought the same."

"You really didn't know until today?"

"I don't know what to tell you except I'm sorry."

For a long while Judy gazed into the liquid green light of a hand-blown lamp, then spoke as if she'd just been dragged from a car wreck. "Tuesdays, when I had my day off, if it was raining, I would go to see Jim instead of you. He gets panicky when it rains, for some reason. I didn't need you to know about him. That's what . . . Don't you see?"

"I guess I don't."

She spoke as if each word had a period behind it. "I don't want to carry around your pity. I'm carrying enough of my own." A tear slid from under her glasses and staggered down one pale, slightly sunburned cheek. "When I think of Jim, I remember the way he was. I love him the way he was. I think

I love you, too, Thomas. But you have such a terrible advantage over Jim. You're on two legs. You're strong. You can talk to me and touch me and hold me. You can make love. You can laugh.

"I wanted us to be friends. And then you messed it up by getting serious. I almost wish you'd been married and unavailable."

I traced a pattern in the carpet with the toe of my shoe.

"You know I can't marry you," she said.

"I think I guessed that from the beginning."

"I can't live with you. It would kill me if any of Jim's old friends saw us together. They'd think he was dead. Can you understand? I have this nightmare: I'm on the street with you, and Jim's mother comes and asks me if Jim is dead. Can you see?"

"I think so."

"But I want you, Thomas."

"You know how I feel."

Judy skated her palms across her thighs, discovered a stray thread in her melon-colored couch, and boxed it with one finger. "I never really dated anybody else. Until you . . . It took Jim a year to tell me he had it, and then it took another year before it got so bad I had to resign my job at Safeco to care for him. We lasted about six months. No money. It was a mess. I nearly went crazy. I technically divorced him, so the state would pay for it all. There was no way we could handle the medical bills ourselves, and the only alternative if we stayed married was for us both to go on welfare and give up everything we owned.

"But he's so proud. He doesn't want me making sacrifices. He told me he didn't love me anymore, that he didn't need me. Said he wanted a divorce. I haven't had the guts to tell him we *are* divorced . . . I don't know why I went out with you, Thomas. I thought you were funny and sweet. I'd been so lonely. Visits to Jim. Work. A short trip to the store. I hadn't seen anybody except the girls on our softball team and the people at work for months.

"At first I thought we could be a one-time thing. I figured sin once and get it out of my system. And then you called again, and you really liked me, and I said to myself, 'Okay, girl, sin twice, and get it out of your system.' You can't know how guilty I've felt. Jim can read me. I know he knows. For such a long time he just kept telling me to go away. Now he doesn't mention it.''

I said nothing.

"Did he see you?" she asked.

"I guess he did."

"He knows then." She touched her hair and crossed her bare arms in front of her breasts; she was having a hard time knowing what to do with herself. "Good. He'd like you. That's good."

A calico cat meandered under some furniture and hopped onto the sofa beside Judy. She stroked it twice and watched it curl up next to her leg. "More than anything I want the picket fence and the marigolds and the children. I'm not making any promises. I'm not even going to promise next week."

"You never have, Judy."

"My brain isn't functioning normally, hasn't for two years. I was thinking with my insides. Seeing you was the most dishonest thing I've ever done. Maybe now we can get to know each other. We were like a couple of pickup artists doing the same pickup over and over. How could you like that?"

"It was you I liked."

"Can I think about it?" She crinkled up the skin around her nose and eyes in a quizzical look and made no move to get up, clearly wanted to bid good-bye from a distance.

"I'll be there."

"Thomas?"

"Yeah?" I was standing by the door now. Stealing a woman from a dying man was a crime I would not commit. If we stayed together, it had to be her decision, as it had been in the beginning. I was not going to plead.

"You're not angry, are you?"

I shook my head.

"You're a good man. Whatever I decide, you're a good man."

I grinned. They always said that when they dumped you. *Vaya con Dios, amiga,* I thought. I would have spoken it, but it was too corny. Besides, neither of us wanted to admit this was adios with a Capital A.

29

MONDAY NIGHT WAS OVERCAST AND windless. We'd divided the watch into three eight-hour shifts, and being the boss, I'd hogged the early one, then come home and ridden my Miyata. I was still too bruised from the fracas with McCline to engage in any weight lifting. I tended some overdue business at Kathy's office, then watched her saunter off to a late dinner with a group of male attorneys. I wasn't invited. I was a detective.

One of the attorneys with a fifty-dollar haircut had bumped into Kathy in the hallway one day and later sent her a note that said she gave "good corridor." Cute.

As the sun dimmed, I stood in the backyard, fussing over aphids on my Sunsprite and powdery mildew on my Troika.

When the phone rang, I ran.

"Thomas?"

"What have you got, Bridget?"

"The girl you found in the Milwaukee with that boy."

"Sonja?"

"She's here with an older man. It stinks all to hell."

Fifteen minutes later I was squatting beside Bridget in a dark window catty-cornered from the Milwaukee. I had stopped only to fetch my wallet and gun and to pull a long-sleeved soccer shirt over my bare arms.

"I think they're inside the Milwaukee," she said. "They went up Maynard Alley. I haven't seen them since."

We focussed our binoculars as the gentle clamor of the street echoed in the room. A restaurant below had opened its kitchen doors, inundating us with the pungent aromas of Chinese cuisine, a concert of banging pots, and a chorus of unintelligible chitchat.

"The man. Who was it?"

"It was already getting dark, and I didn't see him that well. Male Caucasian. Average height and weight. Wore cowboy boots and dirty clothes."

"Tall and lanky? Maybe fifty?"

"Hard to tell alongside her. She's so short."

"Seen anything else?"

"Nothing. But I know it was her. He was holding her arm and propelling her along. She was so scared her knees buckled."

"Call anybody else?"

"The police. I went down and talked to them just before you got here. We couldn't see anything. They said they'd circle a few blocks and keep their eyes open."

"Heard anything on the mikes?"

"Not a peep. I got a picture, though. I don't know if it'll turn out."

"Nice work."

Even as I spoke, our noise-activated tape recorder clicked on, and we heard stirrings on the microphone we'd set up in the west stairway of the Milwaukee: footsteps; shuffling; a man muttering; a girl whimpering.

A girl said, "What did I do? I don't get this shit."

"Just move along, darlin'," said a man.

"I didn't even want to see *you*. You weren't supposed to be there."

"Well, yer seein' me, honey. Now move your little butt."

We heard a squeaky door opening and then two sets of footsteps receding, keys clinking, the door booming closed. A minute later I had decided to go into the run-down hotel myself.

Bridget whispered, "Up there. Look."

Tracing the line of her binoculars, I aimed my 7 x 50s on the same area of the fourth floor she was looking at, focused, and saw something flit past a window. It came back, bright and sparkling and effervescent blue. Years ago the glass had been knocked out of the bottom half of a second window in that room.

A struggle.

Sonja came into view, moving backward, unsteadily, grappling with a man, batting at his hands.

We heard muffled shouts.

Now he was standing behind her, had her elbows folded back like duck wings, pinned behind her, guiding her the way a waiter guides an extra chair for dinner. Sonja balked, disappeared.

We watched the flickering silhouettes as he threw her across the room. I was facing a dilemma: If I ran downstairs, across the street, and up into the Milwaukee, it would take two, probably three minutes to reach them. And I'd generate a lot of noise and commotion doing it. If the man sensed I was coming, he might do who knew what to Sonja. I might never find them.

The scene in my Bushnells mesmerized me.

He had Sonja in his grasp again. I knew there was some-one else in the room because Sonja was wearing a black T-shirt and a dark green skirt and I'd seen blue before. The man wore dull trousers and a work shirt. Sonja was crying, thrashing her legs around in an effort to loosen the man's grip.

Then she went limp.

Slowly she collapsed onto the floor. I was hoping like hell he hadn't broken her neck. He stooped and bent over her prone form. I saw the hump of the man's back as he leaned over his quarry, then laboriously scooped her up, one arm under her neck, one under her knees. Unconscious now, she hung limply in his arms, the mass of her dark hair covering half his side. He carried her to the open window and knelt with her, turning her backside toward us.

He was fitting her through the open window backward.

"Oh, my God!" cried Bridget.

I was glad now that I hadn't moved.

Thumbing the safety off my .45, I braced both hands on the windowsill and told Bridget not to bump my arm. I had already worked a round into the chamber. I couldn't risk a shot at the man. It was too dark, and he was holding Sonja too high, and I hadn't visited the range in years, not since I'd taught Kathy how to shoot.

Placing the upper window into my sight picture, I breathed deeply, let part of it out, squeezed. The .45 made a deafening pop.

Across the street the pane in the upper window cracked and shattered, dripping in large, glittery pieces across the man and girl, mostly the man. In another second or two it would have been too late. Still unconscious, she flopped forward inside the room while he disappeared from view momentarily. He stuck his head around the window, searching for the assailant, then was gone, moving as if he'd had military training. I couldn't tell who he was.

I saw movement in the purplish shadows in the back of the room.

"There are two of them," said Bridget, lost in her binoculars. "One's wearing a costume or something. Blue and flashy. He was throwing her out the window, wasn't he?"

"You carrying?"

"No."

"Call the cops again. Christ, I don't know how they'll find us in that building, but call them."

"Thomas . . ."

But I was gone, grabbing Bridget's flashlight, dashing down the corridor past an elderly Chinese man in his pajamas on his way to the communal bathroom. I flew down two flights of rickety wooden steps and out onto Maynard, the door slamming behind me.

I hit King at a dead run, spun through a group of Asians, almost got clipped by a taxi, and rounded the corner into Maynard Alley.

The odor of moist garbage assailed me. Undisturbed by my panic, a wino slept behind a Dumpster.

All the battered, graffiti-laden, and reinforced alley doors

were locked. I found the one Buzz and I had used and
rammed it with my shoulder, then stood back and kicked. It
was as solid as the brick wall beside it. What I needed was
a crowbar. And time.

Sprinting back out the alley and into the middle of King
Street, I peered up at the Milwaukee. The windows were all
empty.

No.

A flash of black T-shirt. He was in the window again, with
the girl, her limp anatomy perched on the sill, ready to teeter
on a backward trip to hell. I screamed at him, but he kept
on.

I shouted curses, warnings, gobbledygook.

In the street two cars simultaneously slammed on their
brakes. The driver of one car stared openmouthed at the gun
in my fist, glanced over her shoulder to see if she could back
away from this maniac, then frantically slapped down the
locks on all her doors.

I raised my arm and fired four bullets into the glass in
the windows, carefully avoiding the one Sonja occupied. The
gunfire echoed loudly off the buildings on either side of the
street. Sonja flopped out of sight again. A man's head popped
into the window. I airmailed a slug into the bricks beside his
face.

Eyes on the windows above, I crabbed around in circles.
I whooped, and three more cars halted before my macabre
jitterbugging in the street. To stand or to run for it? Whatever
I decided in the next few moments could mean Sonja's life.
I ran back and forth in a zigzagging oblongs, shouting,
"No," at the windows above me and finally I raced up King,
around the corner to Seventh, made my way, gasping, up the
two flights to the Silver Dragon.

Lowering my shoulder and pushing against his chest when
I saw the certainty of our collision, I knocked over a Chinese
waiter. He spilled his tray with a horrendous crash. The restaurant had illegally placed a table and chairs across the
emergency entrance. Four fat businessmen and two fashion-
ably slim wives were dining and joking there.

Before anybody could make a move, I'd capsized the table,

had thrown open the emergency door, and was alone in the stairway. The emergency door closed automatically on the hubbub in the Silver Dragon.

I heard a noise downstairs as a man's face appeared in the doorway of the restaurant four feet behind me. Raising the pistol, I headed down the stairs. The man quickly disappeared back inside the restaurant.

I was a dicey guy with a gun and consequently seldom carried it. I could shoot at people as long as I was certain I wouldn't hit them. I'd done it a minute ago. Yet when it came to life and death, I was not a killer and knew it.

Still, it had saved Sonja's life.

If she was alive. Perhaps she hadn't been unconscious. Perhaps she'd been dead. But who would bother throwing a dead body four stories to a busy street?

I had two choices. Downstairs, somebody was bumbling around in McCline's old offices. Sonja would be upstairs. The footsteps below me were the blundering tread of a man moving fast. I went on intuition. He had to be Sonja's assailant.

As I skittered down the dim stairs, I slammed a fresh clip into the butt of the gun.

I slipped into the dark recesses of the Milwaukee, flicked on Bridget's flashlight, and made my way toward McCline's first-floor offices. I had an unshakable feeling somebody lurked around every corner, waiting to assassinate me.

From McCline's doorway I scoped out the dirtied room and broken walls, using up thirty valuable seconds. Making myself a walking target, I forged my way through the debris, whipping the light this way and that, gun in hand.

The room was empty. The door to the basement was closed.

I stopped breathing and flattened my ear against the paneling of the door. It took a few seconds to figure out what I was listening to: the snort of hyperventilating, thick and phlegmy. My prey was standing less than twelve inches away on the opposite side of the door, catching his breath.

After tiptoeing behind a nearby desk, I crouched and pointed the .45 at the doorway, held the light on it, and said, "Come out of there!"

Shotgun blasts rocked the building, and the door opened in two cookie cutter spots, each the size of a fist.

My ears rang. Just to make sure he knew what he was dealing with, I fired a .45 into the top of the door. I heard boots clumping heavily on wooden steps.

"It's me, Bridget," I yelled at the mike. "I'm okay. He's got a gun. I'm going into the basement after him. The girl must be upstairs still." I didn't want to ask her to—and even if I had, she couldn't have answered—but I was hoping Bridget would take it upon herself to go upstairs after the girl. On the other hand, it was doubtful she'd get through the Silver Dragon at the same speed I had. Even as I thought it, I realized I'd made a mistake coming down here instead of going straight for Sonja.

Standing to one side, I flung open the basement door. A shotgun blast ripped the inside edge of the door, flinging splinters and shot upward into the room behind me. I felt a single pellet dig into my biceps.

When my ears stopped ringing, I heard running footsteps receding into the basement. Shutting the flashlight off, I made my way down. It was so dark I couldn't see the end of my nose.

As soon as I made a noise, he threw two more rounds at me. Five rounds altogether. Few shotguns carry more than five. I listened to see if he was reloading, but what I heard was a large metallic object skittering across the floor, as if he'd thrown the weapon. Muffled footsteps. Grunting. He was already making his way through the wall and into the secret back rooms, in the direction of the tunnel that led under the street. In the dark yet. He knew Chinatown.

There were no obstructions in the tunnel, and when I crouched and waved the light, I could see the rear end and boots of a man hightailing it.

"Stop," I shouted.

Against my better instincts, I bent low and headed in after him.

Though he had half the tunnel length as a handicap, I made better time, for he scooted along the way an old man might. A truck thundered overhead in the roadway. When I reached the opening in the basement on the other side of the street, I heard him making his way up the double flight of steps into the vacant building above. His wheezing lungs sounded like a kid playing with a pump organ. He was out of shape and fading fast.

Breathing deeply, I took the steps two at a time. The only light came from my bobbing flashlight.

Three-quarters of the way up, I tackled him from behind. Before I could pin his legs together, he put a fist in my face. Then he kicked. Bridget's flashlight was gone now, clattering down the steps.

As we climbed to our feet, I pulled at his belt, brought him close in the dark, and aimed at what I thought was his nose. My knuckles made a slick, smacking sound against his face. He moaned and kicked me in the stomach. I kicked back, and before I knew it, we were standing on opposite sides of the stair cavity, kicking at each other like a couple of Girl Scouts. Except he was wearing sharp-pointed cowboy boots and I was wearing Puma running shoes with rubber soles.

When I tackled him again, I clutched him around the chest, threw him into the wall, and then we both went down the steps in a sideways, backward, upside-down tumble. He moaned and sobbed as we hit the sharp edges of each step. Almost at the bottom, there was a hesitation in our momentum, and then he stumbled upward and fell against me, and we both cartwheeled the rest of our merry way to the basement. He landed on top of me and was still.

I pried him off, and as I moved in the dark, a fist landed on the back of my head. I swung the pistol hard and connected against something with a kerchuck. A body fell.

Heavy snoring. He was out.

It took me a few minutes to retrieve my flashlight halfway up the stairs. I returned to the unconscious man. Playing my light on the lumpy shoulders, I grasped him, pulled him around, and studied his face.

30

IT TOOK AWHILE TO PLACE HIM.

Phil Stains. Carstens's desiccated neighbor. Dull brown eyes, half open. Khaki trousers. Cowboy boots with needle-sharp toes and broken-down heels. Flannel shirt so dirty it could have come from the bottom of a rag bin in a service station.

Quickly I tied his hands behind his back with the shoelace out of my left shoe, then left him muttering in the dark on his face. To make certain he didn't wander, I pulled both his boots off and flung them into the darkness. Then his trousers. Predictably he wore long johns.

As I crawled back through the tunnel, gimpy from the drubbing he had given my knees and shins with his boots, it suddenly seemed to me as if Sonja had been alone and unprotected for hours. I hoped desperately that I hadn't blown this one.

I believed I knew approximately where she was: fourth floor on the west end.

By the time I found the room, the blue and red bubble gum machines had finally started their dog and pony show outside. There were a dozen sealed and unmarked doors on this block, any one of which could lead into the Milwaukee. Only three did, and I knew the cops didn't carry the tools to pry them open.

Lying on her side on the floor on the far side of the room, Sonja was semiconscious.

The woman had been bending over Sonja's limp form, trying to tow the girl's body to the window. She didn't have the flexibility or strength.

"Delores," I said.

She straightened up without surprise. She reeked of perfume.

"Where's Clayton? I expected him to be here, too."

"Clay is too innocent to know how the outside world operates. I have always had to take care of things."

Delores wore high heels and a gown that was sequined, aqua-green and gold.

"Let me figure this," I said, moving to Sonja and kneeling. The woman tottered over beside me, stood close behind.

Though there was sufficient light from King Street to see, I played the beam of Bridget's flashlight up into Delores James's face, then turned it on Sonja. I palpated the girl's skull and found a small knot behind one ear, a smear of blood on my fingers. Otherwise she seemed unharmed. Somebody must have . . .

Feeling Delores shift, I ducked instinctively.

It saved my life.

Something hard and fast clipped the back of my head, and I was on my face on the floor next to the girl, watching armies of prickly stars parade past my eyelids. I reached out with one hand and grasped Delores's sticklike ankle. The ankle twisted as she wrenched to escape, but I clawed like a madman. This was it. Do or die. If I let her go, groggy as I was now, she'd kill me.

She was taking potshots at me with a sap. But I was too low for her. And I had her by the foot. It was only when I struggled to my hands and knees that she got in another whack, and then I was on my face.

I was strong enough to move. But move, and she'd nail me again. Spry as she seemed, she apparently found it difficult to bend low enough to give me a good shot where I lay. Maybe it was the dress.

Delores had quelled Sonja with her sap. Must have swung

the same weapon on Todd Steeb. Lured him up here on some pretense, probably telling him she knew the whys and where-fores of his uncle's death and then asked Todd to fasten a strap on her shoe, any pretext to get him into position.

I inhaled the pungent stink of dried pigeon guano, coughed, and wrapped my entire arm around those brittle ankles, using my other arm to shield my skull from her blows. I scooted my knees under my hips and used my entire body for leverage. She got in two solid whacks on my arm before I toppled her.

She went down hard, making a dainty whoopee cushion oomph. I wondered if she'd broken a hip. It took me almost a minute to clear the cobwebs. Besides the thunking in my skull, my left arm felt as if she'd fractured it. I was queasy and beginning to grow sick to my stomach.

When I could stand, I lifted the leather-covered sap out of Delores's fist, watching as her long purple nails raked the air for it. Old-fashioned and handmade, the sap must have been thirty years old, designed for icing pigs and poultry.

"That's my father's," she said.

"Belongs to the city now," I reached down and frisked her, sparing nothing. My arm throbbing, and regretfully I wanted to hurt her.

"What in the world are you looking for?"

"Ice picks, hand grenades, nuclear detonators," She wore a corset. In addition to her surgeries, she had inserted a set of foam rubber falsies, one of which popped out under my rough frisking. It rolled across the floor like an escaped hub-cap and hit Sonja in the face.

When I'd pulled her to her feet, she took a couple of tot-tering steps to road-test the pins and fixed her rheumy pastel blue eyes on me. She knew something vital had upset the geography of her life, but she wasn't quite sure if it was an earthquake or only tremors.

"There was a man," she said. "He kidnapped us."

"Get a better script, lady. You hired Phil Stains to snatch Sonja, just as you probably had his help killing Carstens and Todd Steeb. Jan Galloway, too, I'd bet."

"This is outrageous."

"Let me guess. You met Phil when Carstens needed extra help at your place. He thought you were the most wonderful famous thing he'd ever met. You charmed his socks off."

Lifting her brows and jutting her fine-boned chin, she said, "Philip would do anything for the queen of the silver screen."

"I got news for you. Myrna Loy was the queen of the silver screen."

Her face dropped. "Black. There's money hidden close. Almost a million dollars. It's yours."

I went to the window and hollered at the cops in the street, told them how to get in. I checked Sonja, who was almost awake now. I rolled her over and told her to lie still. Then I rose and pushed Delores against the wall, doing it in tiny bumps, so she wouldn't topple. I couldn't help myself.

"I ought to kill you," I whispered. "I ought to throw you out the window and claim you were coming at me with this and fell." I dangled the brown sap in front of her heavily made-up face.

"You wouldn't hurt an old lady."

"I don't see a lady." Gripping her arms, I pushed my face into hers. "You murdered Todd, damn you."

She didn't reply.

"Okay," I said. "I can see we'll never get any answers. It's just you and me. If it'll work for you, it'll work for me. Out." I gripped her as if I were going to move to the window with her.

The warbling shriek that escaped her throat was as blood-curdling as anything ever laid onto a sound track. I said, "What?"

"I'll talk."

"You've got one minute."

"Sonja knew about Galloway stealing my money all those years ago. She called me. I set her up with Stains and met them here. The money's still hidden. We wanted to make her tell us where, but she was stubborn."

I said, "A distraught teenage lover commits suicide after losing her boyfriend. I'll bet you already have the note written."

The green sequinned handbag on the dusty washbasin

against the wall attracted a guilty glance from Delores.
"We'll leave that for the police," I said. "What about
Todd?"

"He had a filthy way about him. Accused me of murdering
his uncle. I brought him up here to show him. Foolish child.
The money was all mine, you know. Stolen from the trunk
of my car."

"My guess is, you murdered your millionaire boyfriend
Solly McDonald Pucket, and you were transferring some of
the cash. You were probably so nervous you got into an accident. Pucket's relatives thought he kept a lot of cash on
hand, upwards of a million, but they weren't quite sure. Certainly more than they found after his death, which was zilch.
How much did you get from him, Delores?"

"I have done nothing other than what I was forced to do.
He wouldn't marry me because I was an actress. I *earned*
that money."

"Galloway's the one I don't understand. He must have
looked in the trunk of your Rolls-Royce after your accident
and, when he saw what was in it, stole it. Of course, you
weren't going to call the cops. You'd stolen it yourself. But
why not hire a private detective to track it down?"

"Private detectives are known for blackmail," she said.

"Your car had passed through so many hands, the police,
fire, tow operators, people in the yard. It could have been
vandals who broke into the holding yard and snatched it. You
weren't sure who'd taken your money until Jan Galloway
called you six years ago and told you he wanted to give it
back. Bet you didn't know what to think."

She narrowed her watery eyes. "Blackmail. He wanted
more."

I shook my head. "You fool. Haven't you ever believed in
anything good? Haven't you ever known anyone with a conscience? Galloway wanted to give it back. It had been eating
at him all those years. It provided the success every man
hungers for and at the same time became a sad little cancer
on his soul.

"He hid it across the street in the floor of a closet, keeping
it close, then made an appointment with you. Choosing this

particular building must have had something to do with the expiation of guilt. You bashed him and rolled him into the street. For six years it's been sitting across the street in a closet.''

"You're lying," she said.

"That's what makes this all so pathetic. All you had to do was accept the money, but you were too suspicious. Then, when Todd started coming around and you saw the ring on Sonja's hand, you knew it was starting again. You were at his house. The parrot gave you away. 'Am I pretty?' Who else would ask a bird such a question?''

We could hear men clomping down the long corridor, pigeons rustling as the men shone their lights from room to room.

Speaking slowly, enunciating in a protracted dignity she hadn't mustered before, Delores James said, "You cannot harm a legend."

"Watch carefully, babe."

31

TWO WEEKS LATER ON A BLUSTERY June afternoon we sat in Kathy's office, the stained glass windows throwing rhomboids of blues and pinks against Kathy, Sonja, Buzz, and myself. My left arm was in a partial cast.

Delores was sitting in a cell, as was Stains.

I had spent most of the past two weeks tracking down the rightful owner of the fortune.

When I phoned Oregon and got hold of the law firm that had handled Solly McDonald Pucket's estate in 1960, it turned out he had left the bulk of his wealth to an obscure nutty religious organization. Pucket had been senile. The leader of the organization had taken the inheritance and scrammed.

Kathy assured me that if we gave it up, it would end up in the coffers of the state of Oregon. I decided to play God.

I split it fifty-fifty between the two of them, dumped it into a trust, a portion due at twenty-one, the rest at twenty-five, or, prior to that, to finance their educations. Kathy was the executor.

Delores wasn't talking about the money. One, it might link her to Pucket's suspicious death in 1959. Two, she hadn't believed me, refused to think Jan Galloway had planned to return it. It was simply beyond her comprehension.

I had neglected to turn the loot over to the prosecutors, but they didn't need, expect, or know about it. Phil Stains was singing, and they had an easy case without it. Kathy devised a clever way to bestow a trust without making the government suspicious.

We had just finished explaining to Sonja and Buzz about their inheritances. Dutifully Buzz had worn a suit, his hair still in that Mohawk, feet clad in running shoes. In blue-green heels, a tan skirt, Sonja sat primly.

"Wow," said Sonja, leaping off the ship of adult into the waters of child for a moment. "Like winning the lotto, huh, Buzz?"

"Nobody knew you had the money," said Buzz, looking at me. "Why didn't you keep it?"

"Because I didn't."

"Why half to her, half to me?"

"That's the way Todd would have done it."

My statement dampened further objections.

"She really did all that?" Sonja asked. "Delores James?"

"Delores stole the money in 1959, right after she killed her millionaire lover, Pucket. Then she ran away with Clayton. She financed *The Eunuch* with the stolen money. She had tried to get Pucket to finance it, having already gotten a promise from James that she would star. Pucket wouldn't go for it.

"After she killed him, Delores had a car accident with the trunk full of money. She probably was transporting it in small chunks to keep from losing it all in some sort of freak accident, the way she ended up losing part of it. They ambulanced her to the hospital, and your uncle Jan towed the car to McCline's lot on Jackson. When he looked in the trunk, he stole the money and then, to throw off pursuers, forged Chester McCline's name on the towing paper work.

"It was easy enough to catch when I compared the signatures. Six years ago, his business a success beyond his wildest dreams, he decided to give his grubstake back to the woman he believed the rightful owner. He gathered the money up and made an appointment to meet her. Except she knocked him out and had Phil Stains throw him off the roof of the Milwaukee. The money remained hidden until Todd found it. And after Todd, me.''

''Why would Stains help her?'' asked Buzz.

''He was in love with her. She was able to convince him of anything. Six years ago she told him that Jan Galloway was blackmailing her and demanding money, that she had been to the police, and that they had laughed at her. It sent Stains into a rage. Delores contacted Stains again and convinced him Carstens was taking up where Galloway left off. The same with Todd. Delores has charisma. She was able to convince a not-very-smart Phil Stains she's a direct descendant of the pharaohs. I'm serious. He still believes she was being blackmailed, even after the deputy prosecutor told him he'd been snookered.

''When Todd wanted to find out how his uncle really died, he, too, got in touch with Carstens. My guess was Carstens got caught snooping. After I told her I was looking into Carstens's death, she got worried. She'd seen that ring, which had once been hers, on Sonja's finger, and she knew who gave it to Sonja. So she arranged for Todd's 'suicide.' ''

Sonja said, ''When I took you to my dad's offices and you found that piece of paper, I read it over your shoulder. All I knew was Dad towed a car that belonged to Clayton James. She was the driver? I called them up and said some things they probably could have sued me for. I was blitzed. I never even talked to Clayton. The old lady had Stains meet me. He told me he'd kill me if I didn't go with him. He had a sawed-off shotgun wrapped in a blanket.''

''Delores had been lying to me from the start,'' I said. ''The first time I met her she told me she'd never been to Carstens's home, yet she'd just killed him there a day or two earlier. She gave herself away when she said he had horses and a view of the river. You would actually have to go there to know he had a view of the river. It was just a slice, nothing a guy would ever mention. And the horses? He kept those secret because he was keeping them for his nephew, who was hiding them from a divorce settlement.

''Later, when I read Todd's so-called suicide note, something sounded wrong. 'I'm too sorry,' it said. That's a pretentious old woman's phrasing, not a boy's. And it was signed 'Elmore,' not 'Todd.' When McCline knew those words, I thought he'd penned the note. Turns out he got the information from his brother the cop. And your parrot, Buzz. Hitler said, 'Am I pretty?' Who taught it that?''

"Delores? So what'll happen to her?'' Buzz asked.

I looked at Kathy, who said, ''My guess is she'll die in prison waiting for an appeal. The weekly newspapers will have a field day. Local TV stations will play Delores Del Rabo film retrospectives with bars across the *TV Guide* ads. Already *Time* and *Newsweek* are preparing articles.''

"It's not fair,'' said Buzz lowly. ''All these people dead just because of some old lady committing a crime almost thirty years ago.'' Sonja placed her hand on top of his but couldn't think of anything comforting to say. None of us could.

32

AN HOUR LATER I WAS CONFERRING
with Kathy about a business swindle we had promised to
straighten out for a beer distributor when the intercom
buzzed. "Call for Tom," said Beulah.

I picked up Kathy's office phone and punched the lighted
line button. "Black here."

"Thomas?"

"Judy. It's been awhile." Kathy dropped her pencil on the
floor, let it roll under the desk until it hit my foot, gave me
a look, made some signs as if to leave the room, then stood
near the windows when I said, "Don't go."

"Talking to me?" Judy asked.

"Somebody here in the room. How've you been?" Kathy
fluffed her mane of dark hair behind her shoulder and stared
down at Pioneer Square.

Judy said, "I meant to call you, but I haven't gotten around
to it. Originally I was hoping we could get back together."

"Uh-huh."

"That was originally."

"And now?"

"A funny thing happened. Jim died a week ago."

"I'm sorry."

Now I knew the reason for the milkiness in her voice.
She'd been crying. "Yes, well. I've decided to leave town.

Maybe for six months. The owner of the home where I work has another place—in Michigan. I've never been to Michigan. I'm leaving tonight for a vacation in Mexico alone, to sort of recharge my batteries, then on to Saginaw.''

"Need help?"

"There was no funeral. Jim swore he didn't want one. The other arrangements have been made for almost a year. I'm almost through packing. Maybe after some of this wears off, I'll write.''

I didn't know what I was feeling, and I didn't want to make promises I couldn't keep. I had been expecting the worst and hoping for the best, and now she threw me a mud ball from left field.

"Don't say anything, Thomas. I'm not selfish enough to try to extract any promises. If you're waiting when I'm finally ready, fine. If not, that's the chance I take. I love you, Thomas, but I have a lot of thinking to do.''

After I'd hung up, Kathy fixed her jewellike eyes on me and said, "Got a date tonight then?"

"Not tonight."

"There's a new Australian movie at the Egyptian."

I nodded, got up, left the room, and caught the hint of a rueful look. We had unfinished business on her desk. Some months ago Kathy had pronounced my affair with Judy a losing proposition, a deal she said was a clunker from the beginning. I didn't mind people trying to figure me out, but I hated it when they were right.

Downstairs on the street I walked due west until I came to Alaskan Way, then crossed in front of the green and pale yellow electric trolley and stared down into Elliott Bay.

I sat in a tiny waterfront park next to a pair of gentlemen swapping sloppy swigs from a bottle of Thunderbird and listened to the shrill calls of a gull, the tooting of the ferries, the whir of traffic, an occasional car horn echoing off the downtown high rises. I could see West Seattle across the water. An Indian freighter in the bay.

"Thomas?"

"Buzz. I didn't see you."

"I was just walking around trying to figure out why me.''

"Sit down." The boy had unknotted his tie, managing to look disheveled in a suit. "What do you mean?"

"All of it. Almost a half a million dollars. Sonja's on cloud nine, but I don't know how I feel. And my brother. Why me?"

I shrugged. "You ever been running, maybe in the dark, and fall for no good reason? Maybe you stumble over a piece of broken pavement?"

"I guess."

"You might stand there all night wondering, Why me? But that's not what you do, is it?"

"I guess I head on out."

"Sounds simplistic, but what else is there?"

Buzz stared out at the sunlight on the water. "I wanted to thank you for what you did."

"What was that?"

"Proved Todd didn't commit suicide. He's still dead and all, but it made a difference in our family. And my uncle didn't commit suicide either."

"You're welcome."

My thoughts roamed, and I pictured a boy jogging by himself along the shore of Lake Washington. A dead boy without any pictures to remember him by.

"I'll be going now, Thomas," said Buzz.

"There's a seamstress downtown who claims she has Shirley MacLaine's coat in her window. Shirley brought it in to get patched and forgot to pick it up. I thought we could go down there with our cameras some afternoon."

We both laughed. After a few moments Buzz said, "Who's Shirley MacLaine?" We laughed again, almost got hysterical.

After he left the blinding sun sank low enough to ricochet off the pyramids of chop on the sound. I lay back on the stone bench and closed my eyes. I had work back at the office. Kathy would be waiting.

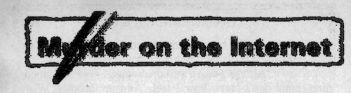

Read the entire Shamus Award-winning
Thomas Black series

from first . . .

THE RAINY CITY

. . . to last:

CATFISH CAFÉ

by

EARL EMERSON

"Emerson is carving his own special niche
among a new generation of private-eye
writers. . . . He writes lean, muscular prose
to carry his fast-moving action."
—*The Washington Post Book World*

Published by Ballantine Books.
Available at your local bookstore.